THE PATRIOTS

THE PATRIOTS

by

JOHN K. DEXTER

A TROJAN PAPERBACK

Published by Trojan Publications – London

Printed in Great Britain

THE PATRIOTS

INTRODUCTION

On February 16th, 1940, the British destroyer "Cossack" entered Norwegian territorial waters and forced the German ship "Altmark" to release British prisoners carried below decks. This incident was sufficient to prove to Hitler that Norwegian neutrality could no longer be depended upon and plans were put into operation for the occupation of Norway and also that of Denmark in order to safeguard the western flank of this thrust north.

Despite British intervention in Norway, both countries were soon under the iron heel of Nazism and throughout the following two years, anti-nazi demonstrations grew in intensity in both countries; Christmas Moller, an active member of the Danish underground fled to England and following his broadcasts to Denmark, the first saboteurs trained in England were parachuted there to lead the patriots and co-ordinate their resistance. In Norway too, acts of sabotage continued against the occupying forces as more men and materials were landed in the country.

This is a unique account of the resistance movements in both Norway and Denmark and in particular of one man who took part in the underground battle against the enemy in both countries. With the emphasis on the bravery, tragedy and humour of the men and women who daily faced internment and death, this is an enthralling and intensely interesting novel of the war in enemy-occupied Europe.

CHAPTER ONE

Prelude

IN the streets, there was the sullen smell of smoke hanging in the air, something foul and threatening. The first wave of bombers had been and gone, dropping their incendiaries, starting the raging fires which would guide the second wave, the main group of enemy planes, the Heinkels and Messerschmitts, to their targets. But at the moment, these planes were somewhere in the distance, just crossing the coast and there was an uneasy silence hanging over London. In places, the fires had taken a firm hold, the light from the blazing buildings burning great red holes in the clouds overhead.

Five minutes later, the sirens blew again. The searchlights probed the darkness of the sky and the clouds with long fingers of brilliance. Now and again, to the south, just beyond the limits of the city, came the intermittent boom of gunfire.

"Are you frightened by air-raids?" asked the man who crouched in the doorway beside me. We had been there for the past thirty minutes, since the raid had begun in earnest. A short, fat man, a correspondent with one of the provincial newspapers, he had talked almost non-stop about every topic under the sun, whether from fear or because it was his usual manner, I could not determine. He had a very serious face, mottled a little by heavy drinking.

"Wll, sometimes it has me worried. I've got to admit it, more especially at times like this when I'm waiting for something to happen."

He nodded to himself, chewing the thought over in his mind. "For myself." He leaned heavily towards me, propping himself up with one hand pressed against the wall. "I find that I sweat and shiver at the same time just as soon as the sirens start. It's as if I'm sure that this time my luck is going to run out on me and that I won't see the morning."

"Then why do you stay here? Wouldn't it be safer in one of the shelters?"

"Naturally." He stared sternly at me. "But nobody can get a decent story down there away from it all. Everything is happening up here. For a good story, the kind that the editor wants, you have to be up in the middle of it all."

The guns in the distance thundered savagely. The first of the enemy planes were almost directly overhead, the beams of the searchlights weaving across the sky, criss-crossing in an attempt to pick out the German bombers.

"Even now, in the middle of the war, all that the people want to read are first-hand stories. The war's moving towards a climax now. You know that; I know it, and everybody in London and Coventry knows it. But there are thousands of people, out in the country, who don't know much about what is going on here. All that they know, they have to read in the papers, stories written by people like me."

He fell silent for a long moment, staring up owlishly into the dark sky, rubbing the side of his long nose. The drone of powerful aero engines hammered incessantly in our ears as we crouched there. At the end of the street, silhouetted against the glare of a burning building, a small group of men, the red light glistening dully on their steel helmets, ran across the street and vanished around the corner.

Suddenly there was a high-pitched whistle which sounded shrilly above the steady drone of the bombers; a sound which grew in volume like a train, hurtling out of a long, dully-echoing tunnel. Desperately, I pulled at the man beside me, throwing myself to the ground. The street heaved beneath my prone body. The explosion crashed against my eardrums, shuddering along the street. There was the sound of a hundred window-panes being hurled out into the street and in the weird, crazy moment before the savage detonation wave brought half of the wall crashing down about us. The air was full of dust and smoke. The terrible explosion rumbled in on waves. More walls broke, more bricks crashed into the street, more dust bit at the back of my nostrils as I sucked in great lungfuls of air. Coughing and spluttering, I clawed my way to my feet. For a few seconds I remained standing, hands over my ears, half-dazed and cursing myself for being out there in the open, instead of with the others, the more sensible people, down there in the Underground.

Slowly, this time, moving with an extreme caution, afraid that any wrong move might bring the rest of the wall crumbling down about us, I edged my way out into the street. For an instant, I could feel my jaws tightening and my nerves panicking again. More bombs were falling in the near distance. Overhead, caught in a cone of searchlight beams, a Heinkel was twisting and weaving in a vain attempt to escape the awful, blinding glare. Worse than staring into the sun, it was impossible for a pilot to look at those great, flaring electrodes and not be completely blinded.

The bursting shells were clearly visible around the plane and it was only a matter of time. Seconds later, the plane was a flaming wreck, falling swiftly out of the sky, the searchlights following it down most of the way. Wrenching my gaze from the scene, I glanced down at the figure of the portly correspondent still lying among the rubble. He had still not moved. Going down on one knee, I turned him over gently and looked at him sharply. The urge to strike a match was almost irresistible. "You all right?"

The other stirred himself, nodded and tried to speak, but no words came through his trembling lips. I lifted his shoulders slightly, trying to make him a little more comfortable. Some of the rubble had fallen across his back and arms when he had hit the ground and I pulled it off him carefully. A bubbling, gravelly cough came from his lips and I noticed with a sudden sense of shock that there were tiny dribbles of blood trickling down his chin from his mouth. I was staggering to my feet in a single instant, looking wildly up and down the street. Then there were feet running along the pavement, pounding on the concrete. Someone shouted something in a harsh, authoritative voice.

Quickly, urgently, I motioned to the man lying in the shadows of the rubble. Two of the wardens went down on their knees in front of him while I stared down over the shoulder of one of them.

The taller of the two ripped the correspondent's coat and shirt away from his chest and shone a hooded torch on to the pale skin. But it was no longer unmarked. I saw the ugly purple bruise along his ribs, down his left side, and my first shocked reaction was how very small and insignificant it looked. Dark and discolouring, but seemingly innocent. Then I noticed the expression on the warden's face as he lifted the man's head.

"It's pretty bad, I think. We ought to get him to a first-aid post right away." He glanced at one of the men standing beside me. "Jack. See if you can get hold of anyone. There's a phone at the end of the road but God along knows if it's still in working order. That bomb they dropped must have landed within twenty feet of here." As the other ran off along the pavement, he went on in a hushed voice: "Bloody stupid fools for staying here anyway. What more do they expect? They've all been warned to keep off the streets during a raid."

He got to his feet, turned to me almost angrily: "Just what were you doing crouched in there? Waiting to see how close Jerry could drop one?"

I shrugged. "I'm afraid I don't know what *he* was doing here, apart from getting material at first hand for some newspaper he writes for; but I have to get to an address along the Embankment."

"Oh, have you." There was a faint note of sarcasm in the other's voice. "Well, I reckon you'd better get down into the nearest Underground and stay there until morning. Unless you're so goddamned anxious to be blown to pieces or finish up like this poor devil here You're damned lucky you weren't killed outright, both of you."

"I know." I said quickly. "Do you think I'm staying here just for the fun of the thing? But I'm acting under orders just as you are. And my orders are to get to this address before midnight. And that little lot up there isn't going to stop me."

"I think I'd better have a look at your identity papers, if you don't mind," said the other, stepping forward.

"Very well." I took out my identity card and the other credentials and passed them over to him, waited impatiently until he had examined them by the light of the hooded torch. Then he handed them back and his manner had changed a little. "Sorry, sir, I didn't realise that it was anything like that." He snapped off the torch. "Very likely this raid will go on all night. You're going to be lucky if you get there in one piece. We've had one or two reports from that direction. It's bad all the way along there."

"That's a risk I'll have to take, I'm afraid." I glanced down at the man at my feet. "But what about this poor devil?"

"Don't worry about him, sir. We'll take care of him. If only we can——" He broke off suddenly. Another heart-stopping whistle, rising to a savage crescendo battered cruelly and frighteningly at our ears. The stick of bombs landed at the far end of the street. There was the unmistakable rumble of masonry crashing on to the pavements, of glass being shattered into a thousand pieces. Once the shuddering echoes had died away, I began to pick my way forward through the darkened street, leaving the small group of men behind me. There was the heavy, pulsing, organised murmur of powerful engines directly overhead; and a deep orange glow from the direction of St. James's Palace. Flames spat upward through the enveloping smoke as I turned the corner and looked down in the direction of the Thames. The street in front of me, wet with the water from a burst main, reflected the orange brilliance of the flames from a million sparkling facets and the gurgling of water bursting upward into the street could be clearly heard.

Without pausing any further, I began to walk swiftly along the narrow street, my shoes crunching the glass fragments so that they seemed to crackle loudly like walking through a frosty meadow. The houses at the end of this street were still standing, almost undamaged: but I noticed that there was, as yet, little attempt to begin organised rescue work among the ruins. That would possibly come a little later, when the chance of survival in the streets was a little higher than at present. I began to curse myself for being an utter fool, for not taking that warden's advice and going down into one of the deep shelters, underground, waiting there until all of this was over. But the orders which I still carried in my pocket had been explicit and there had been an urgency about them which could not be ignored.

The area around St. Paul's was being heavily bombed as I trudged through the ever-thickening smoke which was now beginning to envelop everything. I felt like a stranger, lost in some city which I had never seen before. Here and there, I saw more men sloshing methodically through expanding pools of water as they fought to bring the raging fires under control.

A couple of heavy bombs had landed at the end of this street, plunging through the roofs of two houses before exploding. A car had been hit in front of one of the houses and had been hurled, in a mass of twisted, concertinered metal against a shattered wall. There was the terribly familiar and sad picture of rooms laid bare to the night sky, the walls sliced away cleanly by the blast as though by a knife, revealing the devastation inside. Beds and tables lay strewn in every direction. In the roadway, a child's doll lay, miraculously untouched, undamaged by the catastrophe which had occurred less than five minutes earlier.

I felt a shiver go through me as I quickened my step. The gunfire was now incessant as the enemy delivered the main force of their attack on central London. Stumbling blindly through the swirling banks of choking smoke, I worked my way along winding alleys, heading in the direction of the Embankment. Reaching the Strand, I was surprised to find that only a handful of incendiaries had landed in the area, although the rippling waters of the Thames, dark and muddy, reflected a pink sheet of fire from the burning buildings on the other side of the river.

Here, I came across small groups of men, firemen and wardens, searching for victims of the raid in one or two houses which had been blitzed. For the most part, they looked like old men, their heads bowed; terribly tired men who had known no period of unbroken sleep for many days, men who were now tired to the point of uncaring exhaustion, knowing that they had to continue with their task until they either dropped, or until the pale light of dawn brought a temporary respite. I hurried on without giving them a second glance. A few watched me out of lack-lustre eyes but made no move to stop me as the others had done.

Twenty minutes later, by devious and circuitous routes, I finally reached my destination and made my way slowly up the wide, marble steps. From the outside, the building itself was far from pretentious, giving no indication of the hive of industry and activity which was to be found behind the red-brick walls. There was a flight of stairs leading up to the first floor and another above that which went up to the top of the building. Blinking against the unaccustomed light, I glanced quickly about me. This was the third time I had been inside this place and I was beginning to know my way around. A white card bearing the words 'Typists Pool' hung over a door almost immediately under the stairway and even as I waited, a trim young WRAC came out, looked across at me with a quick arch of her delicately-pencilled brows, then came over in my direction.

"Can I help you, sir?" she asked. Her voice was quiet and precise, and there was a hint of efficient authority in the way she walked.

"Colonel Reddon?" I said, handing over the letter.

She gave it a brief scrutiny, then handed it back, nodding quickly. "We were told to expect you, sir," she said, half-apologetically. Almost involuntarily, she glanced at the watch on her wrist.

"I'm afraid I'm almost an hour late for the appointment," I said grimly, noticing the movement, "but it's sheer hell out there at the moment. I'm lucky to be here at all, to tell you the truth."

"I understand, sir," she nodded concernedly. "If you'll come with me, I'm sure the Colonel will see you right away." She led the way along a narrow, brightly-lit corridor to a glass-panelled door at the far end. There was a shrill whine outside and the floor beneath my feet shuddered convulsively as the bombs exploded in the near distance, but the girl gave no hint of fear or startled surprise as she rapped sharply on the door. Opening it, she stood on one side and motioned me to go in, then closed the door softly behind me as I stepped inside.

There were two men in the room. I recognised Colonel Reddon instantly. The other man was a stranger to me, a civilian, small and of indeterminate age, possibly in his early fifties, with a shock of white hair and wise eyes that looked me over from a broad, ruddy face.

"Well, Major," nodded the Colonel, waving his hand towards the chair in front of the desk. "I see you finally managed to get here. Have any trouble on the way? I believe Jerry is getting a little extravagant tonight. Two raids one on the heels of the other."

"I did run into a crowd of wardens who wanted me to go into one of the underground shelters," I said easily, lowering myself thankfully into the chair and taking the cigarette which the other held out. The wheel of the Colonel's lighter rasped as he leaned over the desk and lit the cigarette for me. Blowing smoke into the air, I settled back into the chair and waited for him to explain why I was there, instead of still with my unit in the North of Scotland.

Reddon nodded and pushed the lighter back into his tunic pocket. "This is Carl Svenson," he said, introducing the civilian. "He'll be one of your constant companions, closer to you than your shadow, from now on so I think the sooner you get to know something about each other, the better."

"Can you tell me why I've been brought here at such short notice, sir?" I asked quietly, after shaking hands with Svenson. "One day I'm in the North of Scotland with my unit, and the next, right out of the blue, I'm told to report here, to you personally. But so far, nobody seems to know why I'm here, least of all myself. Everything seems to have been treated as a top military secret."

"In a way, that's exactly what it is," nodded Reddon. He paused, waited until the shuddering, thunderous echoes of exploding bombs had died away, before continuing. "If the enemy should get wind of this little venture, it could mean all the difference, not only between success and failure, but between your own life and death."

"I'm afraid that I still don't quite understand, sir." I glanced at him in sudden surprise, aware that the civilian was watching me closely from beneath lowered lids.

"You will, but all in good time." The Colonel placed the tips of his fingers together and regarded them silently for a long moment, then said sharply. "You speak both Norwegian and Danish, don't you, Major?"

"Why . . . yes. I was with a Norwegian mining company before the war. Just managed to get out in time on board a fishing vessel. If I'd stayed there another couple of days I might just have ended up in a German concentration camp."

"You're far too modest, Major. From what I've been told, it's more likely that you could have passed yourself off as a Norwegian citizen. You speak the language fluently, you spent more than thirteen years there before you had to leave. I'm quite sure you could have passed yourself off as one of them."

I shrugged, still not quite seeing where this particular

line of conversation was leading, although there was the germ of a suspicion at the back of my mind, slowly crystallising into hard fact. "I suppose that's possible." I admitted finally.

"Excellent. I felt sure that you were the man we wanted, from the very beginning, but I had to be absolutely sure. There's quite a lot at stake here and we can't afford even the slightest mistake."

I waited expectantly for the other to go on but it was Svenson who spoke next. "You know my country almost as well as I do, Major," he said seriously. "For nearly two years now it has been occupied by Germany. They said, when they landed that they had to do it because they could no longer trust in our neutrality, that we allowed British ships to use our waters, that if they did not take over, the British would invade and do so to gain control of our rich mines. Whether or not we believed them made little difference. We could not stand for long against their well-trained soldiers, their tanks and planes.

"But although we were forced to capitulate, we have not given up the struggle. Over the past year or so, the resistance movement there has grown. We are not all like Quisling. There are a great many patriots. What has happened has only strengthened the desire of my people to fight the Germans. Daily, acts of sabotage are carried out, convoys are destroyed in the mountains, vital bridges, roads and stretches of railway are blown up. But this isn't enough. As yet, these are merely scattered and isolated acts. There is no real leadership there, little co-ordination. They need men who have been trained in this kind of warfare, trained saboteurs. That is why I asked that you should be brought here like this."

"I see." For the first time things began to fit together, to make a little sense. "But surely there are a score of men in Britain who have lived in Norway for as long as I have, and who can speak the language fluently. Why pick on me in particular?"

Colonel Reddon smiled faintly. "Because you also

have a few other important assets which the others don't possess. Your training for example has all been leading up to this moment, even though you may not have been aware of it at the time. You're a first-class organiser and that's what they need out there more than anything else."

"I think I'm beginning to get the picture now, sir."

"Good." The other lit a cigarette and went on tonelessly. "For the past five months we've been intensely interested in the activities of the Norwegian resistance movement. We've been shipping in both men and materials, particularly the latter." His voice was as wooden as his expression. There was the crash of bombs outside the building and the lights dimmed appreciably so that it was several seconds before they regained their former brilliance. Colonel Reddon rubbed a forearm over his tired eyes and smiled faintly. "At least, in Norway, you should be away from that, Major," he added flatly.

I flickered a glance at Svenson. The other sat back in his chair, looking up at the ceiling, lost in a seeming indifference, his arms stretched out along the sides. He looked like a man who had started off in love with several ideals, but events had forced him to discard them all; a man who had seen too much for an idealist, and who had no illusions left.

Colonel Reddon caught my glance. He shook his head almost imperceptibly. "I assure you, Major, there's no need to worry about Svenson here. I promised that you should know something about each other. Svenson has been told most of what there is to know about you and it's only fair that I should tell you about him, although in all modesty, he'll no doubt disclaim a lot of what I'm going to tell you. I don't intend to spare his blushes however."

He flicked the grey ash off the end of his cigarette, drew deeply on it for a moment, then leaned forward, hands clasped in front of him. elbows on the top of the desk. His voice was deadly serious as he continued: "Carl Svenson and his family have lived in the small village of

Hayanger for the past two hundred years. Perhaps village is the wrong term here, from what Carl has told me, I gather it's a fair-sized town to our way of thinking. His parents are still there, his father, now well in his seventies, is still resisting the enemy with the limited resources at his disposal. We wanted to pull him out of there when we brought out Carl, but he refused to come. The Germans believe that he is working hand in hand with them, another tool of the puppet Quisling Government."

I knew the area well, had known it for the best part of six years. A picturesque place overlooking the Sogne Fiord against a background of beautiful mountains. But that had been before the Germans had marched into the country. How they had changed the place was something I did not know. They could not alter the mountains or the fiord, for these were things of nature; but they could have changed the minds of the people there, setting family against family, brother against brother.

"When do we leave, sir?" I asked slowly "And what's a little more to the point, how do we travel?"

"That's all been arranged. A plane to the North of Scotland again. From there, you'll go by submarine, reaching Songe Fiord the day after tomorrow. some time around dusk. Everything has been timed and checked as far as possible to the last minute. Things may seem to be a little complicated at times, but I assure you that it's all necessary."

"Necessary for our safety, or so that the enemy won't know anything of our intentions, sir?" I asked pointedly.

He smiled crookedly, tiredly. "Both. Major. It's the least that we can do. Even walls have ears, you know. There have been too many cases of the enemy knowing our plans beforehand. It would be a catastrophe, not only for yourselves, but for our plans, if you were met by the wrong kind of welcoming party when you landed."

The smoke was clearing slowly when Svenson and I

went out into the streets of London again. There was a red dawn brightening in the east and the last of the German bombers had left, the all-clear had sounded and the people were coming up out of the Underground stations once again to face a new day, to bury their dead, to look for any survivors in the ruins, and to try to rebuild their shattered homes before the planes came back once more. Their lives were not ruled and governed by the wailing sirens and the exploding bombs.

Everything went according to a tight schedule. Colonel Reddon certainly chose his men well when it came to running a show such as this. The R.A.F transport plane took off at precisely eleven o'clock and climbed steeply into a cloudy sky. I leaned back, tired, heavy eyes focusing on the scene below us. Through scattered breaks in the drifting cloud, it was possible to make out the terrible devastation caused by the bombing. Whole areas were still burning and smoke hung low over the river, dissipating only slowly Painfully, I eased my body into as comfortable a position as possible in the bucket seat.

"They certainly don't mean you to travel in luxury on these trips." I said thinly, turning to Sevenson.

He laughed and watched the back of the pilot's head through the open interconnecting doorway. "Better enjoy it while you may, Major," he said grimly. "I've an idea that you'll find things more austere once we get on board that submarine and as for when we reach Norway, well. . . ." He shrugged his shoulders and pushed his legs forward, slipping further into his seat.

"I get your meaning." The other seemed almost completely unconcerned. Or was there perhaps a slight frown of worry on his features. "I only wish I'd been given a bit more warning about this. It's something of a wrench to leave an army unit and suddenly find that you're to be landed in enemy-occupied Norway."

The clamour of the powerful engines echoed in my ears as I sat back and tried to relax. A thousand burning questions were still running riot through my brain and although I knew I needed asleep, that this would possibly be the only chance for me to get it, I found it impossible to relax my mind sufficiently and I tried to concentrate instead on the dimly-seen details of the ground below.

"Would you care to go up front with the pilot, Sir?"

I turned quickly, not having heard the soft, cat-footed approach of the co-pilot. Then I nodded. "I'd like to do that very much, so long as I'm not in the way." I got unsteadily to my feet as the plane hit an air pocket and there was the sudden, sickening lurch which brought my stomach up somewhere into the region of my chest. Glancing at Svenson, I saw to my surprise that he had fallen asleep, quite unconcerned with what was happening, his head a little on one side, his mouth open.

Inside the cockpit, the pilot waved me towards the seat beside him. "Take a pew, Major," he said cordially. "This must be a pretty dull flight for you, I suppose. I'm afraid there'll be very little of interest during the next couple of hours, and I thought you might like to take a look at the business end of the plane."

"What about your co-pilot?" I asked, glancing about me in interest.

The other waved a hand negligently. "He's back there somewhere making coffee. I guess you could make use of some."

"Coffee. How in God's name do you manage to get hold of that? Black market?"

"I suppose you could call it that in a way. I assure you that it's the real stuff."

Five minutes later, the young round-faced co-pilot came back into the cockpit, bearing a couple of mugs of steaming coffee on the wooden lid of an ammunition box. I took one gratefully, sipped it slowly. For several minutes, the plane droned on steadily. There was a lot of cloud around and for long periods we seemed to be completely out of touch with the ground.

The plane set us down at a small airfield in the far

north of Scotland, where a car was waiting to take us to the coast. There was no time lost. Colonel Reddon had certainly meant every word when he had told us that there would be a tight schedule for both of us. Beside me, Svenson sat hunched over the map spread out over his knees, peering at it closely in the semi-darkness of the late afternoon. Finally, he lifted his head, nodded in satisfaction and rolled up the map, thrusting it into a battered leather case.

"So far, so good," he said shortly, settling back in his seat. "Now all we have to do is get there."

I checked my watch. It was a little after four o'clock. If everything went according to plan, we were due to meet the waiting submarine in less than an hour. "And then what? I mean, once we hit the Norwegian coast, where do we go from there? Do you have any plan in mind?"

I waited expectantly for the other to answer, but he merely lay back in his seat, watching the grey, misty blur of the surrounding countryside move swiftly past the speeding car in a haze of stunted trees and long stretches of bare moorland. Five minutes passed and still he remained silent, sunk almost in a reverie of his own, scarcely aware of what was happening around him. I opened my mouth to repeat the question, but he suddenly stirred, pursed his lips and said hoarsely: "A plan? It isn't going to be easy, believe me. I was there for several months during the enemy occupation, before I managed to get out of the country. But there are many good patriots still living there, men who will hide us until we can contact one of the resistance bands in the mountains. Once we succeed in getting in touch with them, most of our troubles should be over, although there will always be the danger of discovery. A very real danger especially at this time. The enemy have been moving more troops into the area during the past three months in an effort to stamp out the resistance."

The car purred along the rough, winding roads, carrying us further north into a dim, misty twilight. Here, out in the wilds of Scotland, it seemed difficult to realise that this was a country at war. The scene around us seemed to have changed very little since the days of Bonnie Prince Charlie. Tall, craggy ridges piled up high against the darkening sky on our right, grey slopes parted here and there with the bright silver of falling streams, standing out starkly against the background of glens and high passes.

The driver handled the big car expertly, sitting relaxed behind the wheel. A man, I guessed, who knew every bend and twist in these roads, who had spent all of his life here, as much a part of this country as the lofty peaks themselves.

My watch showed exactly fifteen minutes past five when the car finally turned a sharp bend in the road, dipped down steeply and passed through a pair of iron gates set in the midst of a stretching line of barbed wire. Out of the corner of my eye I noticed the two sentries standing at attention beside the open gates as we passed through.

"Well, Major, here we have it," said Svenson, leaning forward and peering through the window of the slow-moving car. "A nice set-up, isn't it."

I nodded and smiled wryly. We had come upon this place so abruptly, so suddenly, that I still could not take everything in. It was incredible that there could be so large a place as this, tucked away in the middle of nowhere. Long lines of wooden billets with corrugated iron roofs stretched for half a mile in every direction.

WIthin two minutes, we were inside a large room with a fire blazing in the grate. I held out my hands to the blaze and gradually, some of the warmth came back into my body. Behind me, the door opened and a tall figure came in.

"Glad to have you with us, Major," said the other genially, thrusting out his hand and shaking mine enthusiastically. "And you too, Mister Svenson. We'll do everything we can to make you comfortable for the night. I'm only sorry that your stay here will be so short, we very seldom see new faces here, I'm afraid." He gestured towards a couple of chairs, seating himself behind the polished mahogany desk. "I've arranged for a meal to be laid on in ten minutes."

"We'd be very grateful for that, sir," I said, taking the cigarette from the packet which the other held out. "Everything seems to have been done in so much secrecy that nobody has given much thought to feeding us."

"Well now," murmured the other, blowing smoke into the air, "I think we can remedy that. I suppose you can say nothing about why you're here? I know there's a submarine waiting for you, but that's about all I've been told."

I shrugged. "I think the less anybody knows about this mission, the better for all concerned, sir."

"I understand," nodded the other heavily. "Forget I asked. Whatever your mission is, the best of luck to both of you. I've an idea you're going to need it." He glanced at his watch, then rose to his feet, stubbing out his cigarette in the tray. "If you're ready, gentlemen, I'll take you over to the Mess."

About seven in the morning, with a cold wind sweeping down off the rugged slopes to the north—it was still quite dark—we ate a quick meal, and then made our way down to the small quayside where a boat was ready to take us out to the submarine waiting half a mile offshore. The sea was rough and there was a heavy swell running which tossed the tiny boat around like a leaf. "I only hope to God it's a little smoother under the surface than it is up here on top." I said thickly.

Svenson, seated in the stern of the rocking, heaving boat, merely nodded. His face seemed green in the pale half-light, his eyes almost closed in an expression of elaborate exhaustion.

It was becoming lighter every minute. Above us, patches of dark-purple sky showed through the scurrying clouds, driven by a wind which was fast approaching gale force, blowing directly off the rolling Atlantic. I shivered in spite of the thick coat and pulled the high collar up around my face, in an effort to shield it from the cutting fingers of the wind. Around us, the sea was laced with foaming white stremers which stretched away to the distant horizons as far as the eye could see. Every few moments, the boat would be picked up as though by a giant hand, held for an instant poised on top of the rolling billow, before being plunged down, sickeningly, into the trough immediately behind. The lurching, swaying motion was doing things to my stomach which made me regret having eaten so hearty a breakfast. I was beginning to wish that there had been some warning of what to expect.

With every passing moment, the huge waves threatened to curl over us, to crash down upon the coockleshell of a boat and bury it for ever beneath a mountainous weight of grey-green water and foam. For me, the suspense never lifted. My mind was in a perpetual turmoil, wondering if the next sea would send us under, or pitch us so high on its crest that the boat would smash to splinters under the shuddering impact as we hit the bottom of the trough.

By the time we were alongside the sleek length of the submarine, I had scarcely sufficient strength to pull myself out of the boat. I could almost taste the bitterness of vomit in my mouth as I hauled my exhausted body on to the smooth metal hull of the submarine. The ten-yard journey to the conning tower seemed like ten miles as my feet slipped on the water-running hull and the ice-cold gale tore through my clothing, freezing me to the bone. Behind me, Svenson lurched forward, helped by two of the crew. How they managed to keep their feet under such appalling conditions, seemed little short of a miracle.

Down below, away from the bitter cold of the wind, the incessant heaving swell of the sea and the shrieking howl of the gale, everything was in complete contrast. There was no sensation of movement. It was as if the ocean and the wind had ceased to exist. Warmth returned to our frozen limbs, feeling to our arms and legs. I rubbed my chin reflectively, as the Commander came forward to meet us.

"Commander Ramsden, gentlemen," he said cordially. "Glad to have you aboard. I hope you'll make yourselves comfortable until we arrive at our destination." He checked his watch. "We'll be getting under way in ten minutes or so."

"After the journey here, all I need is a warm bunk and a chance to relax." I said quietly. "Strange as it may seem, I'm beginning to wish I was already there. It can't be any worse than the journey so far."

The other smiled boyishly and tugged absently at his magnificent beard. "Just make yourselves at home. If there's anything you need, we'll do our best to provide it, although we can't promise anything."

Once we were under way on the last stage of our journey to Norway, things settled down into a semi-normal routine. Cruising at periscope depth we left the rugged coastline behind and headed north. The muted throbbing of the electric motors provided a background noise which held a curiously soporific quality for both Svenson and myself. While the crew went about their normal duties, Svenson and I seated ourselves in a couple of the bunks not in use and discussed our chances once we landed in Norway.

Svenson cleared his throat softly, glanced about him almost apprehensively, then said quietly: "Three days ago, we were in contact with a small group of patriots who are operating in the vicinity of Hayanger. They were alerted about our arrival and should have made preparations to pick us up and get us away from the shore before any German patrols arrive."

"Can you be certain that the enemy haven't picked up that broadcast?"

He paused for a moment, then shook his head. "Not absolutely, I'm afraid. We know that they have broken some of our codes and have discovered a few of the wavelengths we're using."

I tightened my lips grimly. "So that for all we know, it might be a German welcoming party that we bump into on the beach?"

"It could be. If it is, then there is still the fact that they won't know our code signal. We won't go in unless I'm absolutely certain."

"I hope you're right. It seems to me that you might be assuming an awful lot."

"I know. I'm assuming that the enemy know nothing about this; that there's been no leak of information." Svenson smiled briefly, or perhaps it was merely a grimace, it was quite dark there, "but in a case like this, we have to start somewhere. And remember, I'm risking my life too."

"Of course." I nodded slowly, settled back on the bunk. Over the next half hour, our conversation grew more and more desultory. By now, I guessed that we were well out to sea, making good time, untroubled by the shrieking gale which had lashed the ocean into a heaving, raging swell. It was unlikely that we would be spotted on our journey, unless the enemy had been warned of our plans. I deliberately put that thought out of my mind. The weather was now in our favour; would keep enemy aircraft grounded, especially as far north as this and unless we ran foul of a well-escorted convoy or a destroyer patrol close inshore, there would be little to fear from enemy surface vessels. There was, of course, the faint chance that the enemy had mined the approaches to many of the fiords, or placed anti-submarine nets across them, but that was a risk we would take when we came to it.

Lying back on the bunk, my hands clasped behind my head, I told myself that Commander Ramsden was a man who knew what he was doing, had probably made a run like this many times in the past, and knew these waters like the back of his own hand.

Time passed slowly. Several times my eyes closed and I fell into an uneasy doze, the gentle humming of the motors, throbbing in my ears, drugging my mind until it was impossible to keep awake.

I was awakened by someone shaking me urgently by the shoulder. With an effort, I forced my eyes open and eased myself painfully into a sitting position. My right arm felt numb where I had been lying on it but a moment later, I was fully awake, focusing my eyes on the man who stood beside me.

"The Commander's compliments, sir," he said softly. "He'd like to see you right away."

I swung my feet to the floor, noticed that Svenson was already awake, waiting for me. Slowly, we made our way for'ard. The Commander stood at the periscope, his arms resting loosely on the grips, eye glued to the lens. At last he straightened, motioned me forward.

"We've run into the middle of a Jerry convoy, Major," he said without a trace of concern in his tone. "Care to take a look for yourself?"

Nodding, I went forward, peered through the periscope. At first, I could see nothing. Then, gradually, my vision became accustomed to the dimness and I was able to make out the slender shapes of two German destroyers about three quarters of a mile away, moving slowly from right to left.

"Is there any danger that we might be discovered?" I asked tightly, looking across at the Commander.

"There's always that possibility," he agreed. "This convoy is larger than any I've encountered in these waters before. Probably iron ore being taken south to Germany. We're still the best part of thirteen miles from the coast. In fact, I would hazard a guess and say that——"

"Enemy destroyer approaching fast, sir," shouted someone in the background. It was a young, excited voice which broke in on the Commander's explanation.

Somewhere in the distance, above the muted throbbing of the motors, there was a sharp pinging sound which I noticed for the first time, but which must have been there for almost a minute.

"Asdic," said the Commander as I turned my head quickly Then, more sharply and urgently: "Stop engines."

Evidently, there was no time to submerge further. I felt the muscles of my stomach tighten in tensed expectation. The pinging grew louder, each individual sound beginning to run into the next. The enemy ship was very close now and a few seconds later, I could hear the muted sound of propellers threshing the water overhead. To my strained senses, it sounded as if the destroyer passed within ten feet of the submarine, lying motionless and silent in the water. My mind told me that it only needed Asdic on the enemy ship to pick out our position, or the sharp eyes of a look-out to spot the faint triangular wake of our periscope, or the periscope itself, and we were virtually finished. Never in the whole of my life had I felt so afraid and helplessly tensed.

In the submarine itself, no one spoke and I had the unshakable impression that every single member of the crew was holding his breath, trying to still the thudding of his own heart against his ribs for fear of the sound being somehow transmitted through steel and water into the ship moving overhead.

Seconds lengthened into a nerve-wrenching eternity. Very slowly, painfully so, the pinging of the Asdic regained its normal strength, the signals well spaced. The sound of propellers could no longer be heard. Men breathed easily once more, and I saw them looking at each other with the eyes of men who had thought to look upon death—and very soon.

Commander Ramsden exhaled slowly, took another quick, all-embracing look through the periscope, then stepped back. "Down periscope," he said harashly. "I think it's time we got the hell out of here. There are too many German destroyers out there for my liking and the next time we may not be so lucky."

"It's a pity you can't use a few of your torpedoes, Commander," said Svenson softly. "It must be highly frustrating to sit here and not be able to sink one of those ships out there."

"There'll be other times for that, Mister Svenson," said Ramsden pointedly. "For this particular trip, all of our energies are to be devoted to putting you safely ashore and landing our cargo of supplies without them falling into enemy hands."

An hour later, the German convoy had disappeared over the horizon and outside, it was growing dark as the short, northern day drew rapidly to its close. Slowly, we edged our way along the shore, gradually approaching the entrance to Sogne Fiord. Very slowly and carefully, engines running at half throttle, we entered the fiord in almost pitch darkness. Even under the best conditions, it would have been a tricky navigational business, but in virtually total darkness, ever on the look-out for patrolling vessels or coastal batteries, it was ten times more difficult.

We surfaced shortly after nine o'clock, some three hundred yards off the rugged coastline. Overhead, the sky was clear and frosty, covered with a bright powdering of stars and there was a crescent moon low on the western horizon, adding a little light—sufficient for us to make out details of the coast in the distance.

"They ought to be there by now," said Commander Ramsden firmly, turning to one of the crew. "Send the signal."

For a moment, there was silence apart from the clacking of the Aldis. We waited, with the icy wind swirling about us, chilling us to the marrow. Every pair of binoculars on the bridge scanned the darkness directly ahead. There was nothing to be seen, just nothing at all. Beside me, Svenson's face was silent, expressionless. Then, abruptly, on the shore, there were sharp flashes of light.

CHAPTER TWO

Night Landing

SVENSON stood like a man carved from stone beside me, oblivious to the bitter, cutting swirl of the wind that whipped around us, to the salt spray which lashed over us, drenching us to the skin, stinging our eyes and flesh like a thousand sharp-edged knives. He had the spare pair of binoculars which the Commander had handed to him, clamped tightly against his eyes.

"Looks to me like your signal, Mister Svenson," said Commander Ramsden harshly, raising his voice a little to make himself heard above the banshee shriek of the wind. "Does it check out?"

"Perfectly, Commander." The other lowered the binoculars and looked down at the luminous watch on his wrist. "How close will you be able to take us inshore?"

"Not much further, I'm afraid. For all we know, they may have batteries out there on the headland. It only needs a couple of searchlights to pick us out and we would be sitting ducks."

"I see." The other turned in my direction. "It looks as though we're in for a rough crossing again, Major," he said humourlessly. "I had hoped not to have to go through that again."

"If there's nothing else for it, we'd better go."

"We'll have everything loaded on board within ten minutes." The Commander gave a brief order. "There isn't much on this trip. A radio, batteries, some weapons and ammunition, a case of plastic explosive." His voice held atouch of grim irony as he went on tersely: "I think you'll find that if they need any more, they have their own ways of getting it."

Four men were busy loading ammunition and equipment

into the large dinghy which bobbed up and down against the smooth hull of the submarine. By now, the heavy swell, running alongside the submarine had most of the hull awash and it seemed incredible that men could work so efficiently under such appalling conditions. Cat-footed and silent, completely co-ordinated, each man seeming to anticipate the moves of the others, they worked swiftly; dark figures some twenty feet away, barely seen in the darkness.

I pulled the thick collar of my heavy coat up higher around my face in a vain attempt to shield it from the wind.

"The moon will be gone in less than half an hour," remarked the Commander suddenly, "at least the darkness should hide you from any Jerry patrols. They won't be expecting anyone to attempt a landing on a night such as this." He turned to Svenson. "You won't find it easy to beach the dinghy in one piece. There are few places along this coastline where you can land in safety at the best of times and with a swell like this running, it's going to be a thousand times worse. I trust you know this area well, Mister Svenson; for your own sakes."

"I've lived here almost all of my life, Commander. I could beach that dinghy with my eyes shut on a night darker than this." There was neither bravado nor boasting in the other's voice. It was merely a statement of fact. He meant every word that he said.

The four men came up on to the bridge from the water-running hull. Everything was ready for us. Commander Ramsden checked his watch again, then shook hands with both of us.

"I suppose it sounds a trifle banal to wish you both the best of luck," he said quietly, "especially when you're going out into that." He jerked his thumb in the direction of the heaving swell of the sea which stretched between us and the towering peaks overlooking the fiord, "but you'll be needing every ounce of luck you can get from now on." His teeth showed faintly as he gave a brief smile. "Rather you than me, gentlemen. At least you both know the country and the language and I can assure you that your papers are accurate to the last detail."

He made to say something further, hands gripping the rail in front of him, but at that precise moment, there came the unmistakable sound of gunfire echoing across the sea, followed by the dull thud of a heavy explosion. Almost simultaneously, a searchlight snapped into being further along the coast, possibly four or five miles distant and began weaving erratically in the darkness.

"Looks like trouble, Major," said the Commander sharply. "I think you had better get under way before anything else starts."

Scrambling, lurching, feet slipping on the greasy surface of the hull, we made our way for'ard to the dinghy. Climbing on board, we pushed off from the submarine and began paddling strongly in the direction of the coastline. Less than ten yards from the curving hull of the submarine, the tide caught us and we began to move swiftly, the waves coming in at us diagonally, battering fiercely at the dinghy so that it spun like a top, caught by forces which threatened to rip it apart at the seams. And there was now an added danger.

Steering the unwieldy dinghy was virtually impossible with the seas fine on the port quarter and a regular succession of high waves and troughs smashing into us continually and at times, quite unpredictably. Time and time again, water came pounding over us in a drenching spray, so dense that it often threatened to engulf us completely. For Svenson, crouched in the bows, trying desperately to peer through the curtain of spray, it must have been a terrible ordeal, the salt water lashing viciously across his face and eyes, eyes which were so terribly vital now if we were to beach the dinghy safely and at the proper point.

I tried to see his face, to make out the expression on it, but through smarting, tear-brimming eyes, I could make out little more than a pale, grey blur and deep-sunken eyes. Not once did he turn his head, even when a curtain of sea water smashed into him. Once, he staggered as the boat climbed almost vertically to the top of a curling crest, hung there for one terrible instant before plunging down again in a bone-slamming descent that seemed to carry us down to the very bed of the ocean.

God, I thought sickly, how could anyone expect a man as old as this, to stand up to such physical and mental torture? Gradually, the ice-cold spray numbed my body. There was now no feeling in my arms and legs, my fingers were clenched tightly around the shaft of the paddle, but I could not feel it. Only once did my mind wander from what was happening at that moment; when I tried to figure out, in a detached way, the reason behind that explosion and the chatter of gunfire which had preceded the appearance of the searchlight further along the fiord.

A lifetime seemed to tick agonisingly by. In the distance, it was just possible to see the line of white foam which marked the coastline of the fiord. Even above the continuous roar of the wind shrieking in our ears, it was possible to hear the thunder of surf crashing on to the base of the towering rocks. They rose high above the water, climbing sheer into the dark sky, the tops touched with the last rays of the moonlight. Hayanger itself, lay at the head of a tributary of Sogne Fiord and we were now passing between rising walls of rock. Svenson moved a little further into the dinghy, his hands white-knuckled on the sides, head high. We looked at each other in silence for a long moment, white-faced. The dinghy shuddered as a huge wave picked us up and hurled us forward. The roar of surf was deafening in our ears and I had the impression that we would be smashed like a cork on those unyielding pillars of rock.

"Do you think we'll make it?" I yelled at the top of my voice. There was no possibility of any Germans in the vicinity hearing us, not above the continual thunder of surf and wind.

"We'll make it all right." His words were whipped from his lips by the wind and torn away so that I barely caught them. Then there was no time to think, time only to act instantly and instinctively, to pull hard on an oar which seemed to have a life and a will of its own, to ignore the pain of a bruised and battered body, of a brain that refused to take in everything. Svenson, seated on the opposite side of the dinghy, his face white and etched with the strain, was pulling hard on the other oar, trying desperately to hold the bobbing, swaying dinghy on course. Everything, the success of our mission, our very lives, depended upon him picking the right spot in the almost pitch darkness, of guiding the frail craft towards it and holding it there.

Then, suddenly, we were running straight before a stern sea and the dinghy was amazingly steady. All at once, I realised just how much this man knew of the sea, of the raging waters which could be found in the fiord, how he knew possibly more than any other man. It seemed incredible that he could have known of this, it must have been a sheer impossibility to see that far ahead.

But Svenson had known this stretch of ocean for close on fifty years. knew its moods and its temperament. There was a long moment of comparative calm with the shrieking wind passing high over our heads as it swept up the lee of the tall mountains. We were now less than fifty yards from the line of white foam and the distance was closing rapidly.

"Nearly there, Major." Svenson's voice was calm and precise, without the slightest trace of exhaustion. I raked a glance over his shoulder. By straining my eyes to the utmost, it was just possible to see a shallow, curving bay, backed by the tall mountains. Ten seconds ticked by and then, abruptly, almost without warning, the dinghy shuddered, there was a sudden impact which sent me sprawling helplessly on top of Svenson. My numbed mind barely grasped the fact that we had hit the shore. For several moments, I lay there, all of the wind knocked from my body, my soaked clothing clinging to my skin with an icy touch. Then I was aware of Svenson speaking swiftly, urgently, his voice muffled a little as he struggled to extricate himself from beneath the weight of my body.

"Are you all right, Major? You are not hurt?"

"No, bruised all over and my lungs seem to be crushed, but apart from that, I'm fine." I pushed myself to my hands and knees with a tremendous physical effort, remained in that position for what seemed an eternity, gasping air down into my aching lungs. Bending, Svenson grasped me tightly by the arm and hauled me upright so that I stood swaying for several moments, blank-faced, staring in front of me into the darkness. But even then, with every nerve and muscle in my body demanding rest, some spark of discipline in my tired brain told me that there was still work to do, that we had to unload the dinghy and get all of the equipment on shore before any German patrols could happen on the scene.

Less than five minutes later, when we had all of the ammunition, weapons and other supplies piled in a neat heap on the rocky strand, we heard a faint sound in the near distance, the sound off footsteps moving towards us, the footsteps of several men. Instantly, we froze close to the dinghy pulled up on to the sand. The reassuring weight of a pistol in my right hand, I peered intently into the darkness, trying to discern the approaching figures, my finger bar-straight on the trigger.

A German patrol—or some of the villagers? It was, as yet, impossible to tell. Within a few seconds, however, it became obvious that whoever it was, they were searching deliberately for us, that they knew we were there.

Something moved at the very edge of my vision. Swiftly, I jerked my head towards it, but it had vanished again. Remembering the first essential of seeing faint shapes in the almost total darkness, I moved my gaze slowly from side to side, realising that under conditions such as these, averted vision was by far the sharpest and most reliable. The dim shape swam back into focus. Two more joined it and came forward at a silent trot.

"Don't shoot," hissed Svenson urgently. "These are the men we came to meet."

Very slowly, still not sure of myself, I got to my feet as the others came towards us out of the darkness.

"Carl?" The voice was soft, barely audible.

"Yes. This way." Svenson stuffed the pistol back into his belt. There was a sudden relaxing of the tension and I sucked in a deep breath as five dim figures crowded around us. Three of them carried rifles, the others had pictols in their hands.

The tallest of the men, obviously the leader of the small band said something in a low undertone to Svenson, then nodded his head, clearly satisfied.

"This is Aasmund Tvedt, one of the leaders of the Resistance Movement in this area," explained Svenson briefly. He turned back to the other and went on: "This is Major——"

"No." Speaking swiftly in Norwegian, the other said harshly: "There will be no English names here. It is far safer that way. We will know you only as Henrik Björnson, the name on your papers."

"That suits me." I acknowledged. "You know why I'm here, I suppose. To help co-ordinate the resistance movements in this area, to train men how to make the most use of their arms and equipment."

"We understand all of that," nodded the other. "But first, we must get all of this equipment away and destroy the dinghy. Doubtless you heard the gunfire to the east. Unfortunately, the enemy have stepped up their patrols in this vicinity during the past two days. It was impossible to warn you of this and we were forced to create a diversion. By now, they probably suspect what has happened and they will be heading in this direction as quickly as they can. I ordered the rest of the men to pull back after half an hour of fighting."

"So that's what all of the shooting was about," I said softly. "We ought to have known." My mind was beginning to function normally once more, although my body was still numbed by the wind which, aided by my wet clothing, lowered the temperature of my body several degrees.

Tvedt gave an order and the pile of equipment was divided quickly into four parts. Unhesitatingly, the men gathered it up and moved off into the enveloping darkness. Now there remained only the dinghy to be disposed of. This was done quickly and efficiently by digging a four-foot deep hole in the soft sand, very close to the water's edge, burying the deflated dinghy in it, patting down the sand firmly.

"Once the tide comes in and then goes out by morning, it will have removed all traces of that," said Tvedt confidently. Turning, he led the way over the rock-strewn beach, towards the silent town which lay in darkness in the distance.

Now that we had arrived, that we had survived that terrible crossing from the submarine, I felt like a man who had been suddenly and unexpectedly reprieved from death and yet there was no sense of thankfulness within me. I felt tired and terribly empty as if my body were only a shell and the living, feeling part of me had been left behind, somewhere along the weary length of months and miles.

We moved forward noiselessly, following Tvedt as he picked his way unerringly through the pitch blackness. Gradually, as we progressed, the going became more difficult and we were forced to halt several times, crouching in the bitterly cold wind which swept down the mountain slopes and cut through our clothing like a knife. After a while, we began climbing into the darkness Inside me, I felt a keen sense of unrest. It was difficult to realise that the Germans were all around us, that we were inside enemy-occupied territory and that if we were caught, there would be no chance of internment, of being treated as a prisoner of war. We had no uniforms. If we were captured, we would be treated as spies, tortured possibly by the Gestapo and then shot.

Tvedt paused and motioned us down with a swift wave of his hand. I went down on one knee, my brain so numbed with exhaustion that I scarcely cared what was happening. Beside me, Tvedt had taken out his pictol, holding it balanced carefully in his right hand, shoulders hunched forward as he peered into the night. Then I heard it. The crackle of heavy boots on frosty earth.

"A German patrol," hissed Tvedt, pressing his lips close to my ear. "Over there in the gully."

I glanced in the direction he indicated but at first could see nothing. Then, as my eyes grew accustomed to the unfamiliar angles and depressions, as contours and shapes swam into focus out of the background, I saw the small group of men struggling up the steep slope. They carried their rifles across their backs and although clearly alert, did not seem to be deliberately looking for trouble.

They passed within ten yards of our hiding place and it was possible to hear the harsh gale of their breathing as their feet stumbled and slipped on the treacherous ground. Not until the sound of their footsteps had faded completely into the distance did we move again.

"We were fortunate," whispered Tvedt quietly as he moved beside me. "They must have been near the end of their patrol. If they had been just starting out, they would have been more careful, more watchful. Probably they were thinking too much of getting under cover in front of a warm fire, than of looking for patriots in the darkness."

"How much further do we have to go now?" murmured Svenson, as he laboured along the slope behind us. "I don't think my legs will carry me much further."

I turned quickly and caught hold of his arm, helping him forward. For an instant, his body sagged heavily against me, then he pulled himself together and smiled feebly. His face looked ghastly in the darkness, drawn into harsh lines of strain. For the moment, I had forgotten the way in which he had guided that dinghy into the shore, the battering his bruised and weary body must have taken from those terrible waves which had washed over the frail craft, hammering against his flesh as he had knelt in the bows. God alone knew how he had managed to keep up with us this far, I reflected.

"We will soon be there," said Tvedt confidently. "Another quarter of a mile perhaps. But we must keep moving. Do you think you can make it?"

"Yes, I'm all right. I thought at first, you might be taking us up into the mountains."

"No. There is a small school in Hayanger. The teachers there can all be trusted implicitly. It will be safe for you to remain there for a few days until we can move you out to a more secure hiding place. Then will come the most difficult part. As soon as possible, we must introduce you into the life of the town. Your papers have all been prepared for you, I presume?"

"Down to the last detail." I assured him. "There's nothing to fear on that point."

"Good. Perhaps it will be easier than we have anticipated. The weapons and ammunition which you brought with you, will be taken to a hiding place in the mountains. There it will be safe, even from the Germans."

Gasping in the bitter, sub-zero wind we fought our way along the narrow winding road which led into Hayanger. There were no more alarms. There was one bad moment as we reached the outskirts of the town when Svenson, staggering alightly, fell against a tall wooden fence in front of one of the darkened houses which rattled loudly like a shaken tarpaulin and there was an instant of sheer agony, of suspense, as a dog inside the house began barking furiously. But after a long wait with tightly-held breath, there was no sign that any Germans in the vicinity had noticed anything, and we moved on again.

We reached the school after twenty minutes of creeping and crouching. Tvedt led the way in. The classrooms were in total darkness, rows of empty desks arranged in neat lines.

"What about the pupils?" I asked tensely. "How can you be sure that none of them won't talk, perhaps to their parents. There might be some Quislings here."

"None of the pupils will ever see you." The other opened a door at the end of a long corridor and motioned us towards it. "You will be down below in the cellars under the building. There is another way out should the Germans decide to carry out a search of the place, but that's unlikely."

Cautiously, I followed him down the stone steps which led into a pit of almost stygian darkness. Our footsteps echoed eerily around us as we reached the bottom. There was a table in the middle of the cellar and Tvedt lit a lamp, setting it in the middle. By its light, I saw that there was some furniture there and it had clearly been used several times in the past. For hidding escaping refugees hoping to make their way across to England, or perhaps Sweden? I wondered. Or sinply as a temporary headuarters of the resistance?

Tvedt answered my unspoken question a little while later, when we were seated around the table, surveying each other by the flickering light of the hurricane lamp. "You're probably wondering at the relative comfort of this place, considering that it's nothing more than a cellar. The truth is that we sometimes have to hide people in a hurry. There are still several important men in Norway that the Germans would dearly love to lay by the heels, men who can be of very great value if they can be smuggled out of the country and across the sea to England."

"Political refugees," said Svenson casually, nodding.

"Mostly. Some of them are scientists." Tvedt leaned his elbows on the table and eyed us in turn. "I know very little of such matters myself. I am merely a fisherman. As far as the Germans are concerned, that is all that I am. I know nothing of science or politics. But I do know that some of the men who have passed through here on their way to freedom have taken with them information of great importance and value to the Allies."

"'And the Underground Movement in this part of Norway," I persisted, changing the topic of conversation.

"What of it? That is mainly why we are here. At the moment, according to information reaching London you're operating mainly in small groups, blowing up a few bridges here and there, wrecking enemy troop trains, and generally making a nuisance of yourselves as far as the enemy is concerned."

The other nodded heavily, shrugging his massive shoulders. "That is all that we know how to do, Major. A thousand pardons. I should have said—Björnson. We need weapons, ammunition, grenades, explosives. The men have the will, the desire to fight. But without arms, without the proper leadership, we can do very little. That is why we looked forward to your coming."

"How many patriots are there within—say, fifty miles of Hayanger?"

The other pursed thick lips, his brow furrowed into lines of concentration. "That isn't easy to say. Three, perhaps four, hundred. As you can realise, we must be careful. The smallest mistake could mean the capture of many men. And once in the hands of the Gestapo, someone may talk. They have their methods of getting the truth from stubborn prisoners, and some of the men working with us, although loyal Norwegians, are old men and young boys. They would talk in the end and what they could say might mean the end of an entire resistance group.

"Then, too, the enemy have been known to take hostages as a reprisal against acts of sabotage." His voice dropped a little in pitch as he went on slowly: "It isn't easy to explain to a sixteen-year-old boy that he must continue to fight on, even though by doing so, it will mean that his father and mother will be shot in the town square by a German firing squad."

"Has that happened here?" asked Svenson sharply. Some of his initial weariness seemed to have evaporated and there was a tenseness about him, about the way he spoke and held himself, which I had never seen before.

"Not in Hayanger. But we have heard that it has happened in several of the other towns nearby. Perhaps we have been luckier than the rest." The bitter irony in Tvedt's tone was clearly audible. He sat quite still for a long moment, staring straight in front of him, then pushed back his chair and rose lithely to his feet. "I must go now. Sometimes, the enemy make lightning checks throughout the town and if I'm discovered to be missing after curfew, it will be difficult to explain things to the German Kommandant."

"Of course." Svenson rubbed the back of his band over his forehead in a gesture of weariness. He got unsteadily to his feet, went over to one of the low bunks ranged against the far wall and threw himself thankfully down on it.

Tvedt hesitated at the door, turned back. "In the morning, whatever happens, stay down here. No one must see you. I shall come along about nine o'clock and we will discuss the position more fully." He jerked his thumb in the direction of the small cupboard in one corner. "You'll find some food and drink in there. It isn't much, but now that the Germans have occupied our country, we are a poor people. It will not always be so. One day, the day of liberation will come, but until then we must wait and fight as best as we can."

He closed the door gently behind him. Getting to my feet, I bolted it, sliding the well-greased bolts into place.

"Better get some sleep while you've the chance," murmured Svenson sleepily from the other side of the room. He stretched his body out luxuriously on the bunk, hands clasped behind his head. "This is what I've looked forward to for the past two days. Now everything seems worth while."

I was wakened the following morning by the sound of footsteps on the ceiling over my head. For a long moment, my mind groped blindly, trying to orientate itself. Then memory came flooding back and I sat up in the narrow, low bunk, rubbing the muscles along the back of my neck gingerly. Checking my watch I saw that it was almost eight-forty-five. There was scarcely any light in the cellar and a cold dampness assailed me as I swung my legs to the floor, stood up and stretched myself luxuriously. Svenson was still asleep on the other bunk, one arm flung over his chest. I shook him by the shoulder.

He was awake in an instant. "Tvedt should be here in fifteen minutes." I said quietly. "Sounds as though school is just beginning."

He nodded. "No one will come down here," he said confidently. "Besides, Aasmund will have had everything planned for days. The only thing that worries me is the diversionary attack they were forced to make last night while we landed. The Germans are not fools. It won't take them long to figure out what lay at the back of that attack."

"And then they'll intensify their search. Is that it?" I asked. Going over to the cupboard, I took out a small loaf and a flask of crude wine.

"Naturally. They must be worried by now about the mounting scale of the resistance. Norway is important to them. Not only strategically, but because of the iron ore they need so desperately. Besides, they're busy trying to build up a reputation in the Far East, hoping to win over new allies. If they show that they can't keep their own house in order in the countries they already occupy, it isn't going to be easy to win over anyone who is still a little unwilling to come down off the fence of neutrality."

"That makes sense, I suppose." I chewed reflectively on the dry bread, washing it down with a little of the fiery-tasting wine. It was now possible to pick out the sounds of more and more children arriving at the school. In spite of Aasmind's assurances, I expected at any moment to hear a sharp, authoritative knock on the thick wooden door and to hear a voice shouting in German for admittance. But no one came. In the school itself, the sounds of activity gradually settled down to an occasional shuffle above us. Lessons had begun and we could expect Aasmund at any moment.

He came five minutes later, bolting the door after him. Heaving a small pack on to the table, he said roughly: "There. I think you'll find that food a little more to your taste."

Opening the pack, I found inside several slender bottles of wine, the real McKay; some cheese and white bread.

"From the German Kommandant's kitchen," explained Tvedt, with a touch of pride in his voice. "I'm quite certain that pig will never miss it."

"But how in God's name did *you* manage to get your hands on it?" muttered Svenson, wolfing into it.

"There are ways and means," said the other mysteriously. Then his face brightened. "But to tell the truth, one of my most trusted men works in the Kommandant's kitchen. As far as they are concerned, he is the best chef in the area, and one of their most loyal supporters. In reality, he is one of us and keeps us supplied with important information. If the enemy only knew how we know beforehand when and where their troop convoys will go from here, or when we can expect a train laden with iron ore, there would be an immediate vacancy at German Headquarters."

With something inside my stomach, I felt better. Things weren't going to be so bad after all, I thought calmly; Here we were, inside Norway and as far as we knew, the enemy did not have the slightest inkling that we were there. Now it only remained for us to establish ourselves as *bona fide* members of the community and the first part of our mission would have been successfully completed.

Then Tvedt said softly: "Tonight, you will meet all of the members of this resistance group. You will explain to them what your plans will be, how you intend to go about co-ordinating the various groups, welding them into an efficient fighting machine. I warn you now that it will not be easy. Even though we are fighting the same enemy, there is fierce rivalry among the individual groups and the leaders of each will not wish to relinquish their command and work under a stranger, taking orders from him. They are all proud men. So far, they have given the orders to the men under their command. I myself, would not wish to give up my position as head of this group, but if it is essential, if it will mean that we shall kill more Germans at a lower cost to ourselves, then I am willing to do so. But you must understand that I cannot answer for any of the others."

"I realise that." I said thickly. "There is no question of them having to relinquish their individual commands. That isn't why I am here at all. As for having to take orders from me, that will only be for a little while. You know yourself that most of them are not military men. They are fishermen such as yourself, carpenters, or men who fought in the First World War when tactics were vastly different from what they are now. All that I want to do is to train them as far as possible in the ways of guerilla warfare. To be really efficient, you must work together, plan your attacks, sabotage vital targets—which are not always those you consider to be of strategic military value to the Germans."

The other pondered this for a long moment in silence, then fixed me with a direct stare. Nodding, he said: "Very well. I understand. There is only one thing that matters, one thing which is above personal pride and egoism. The destruction of the enemy. Everything must be directed towards that one end."

"Now you're talking." I acknowledged. "What time do we meet the others—and where?"

"At six o'clock tonight. Five miles north of the town. I will take you there myself. There is just one thing."

"Yes?" I looked at him curiously.

"It has been snowing thickly for the past three hours. By tonight, there will be snow everywhere and it will be necessary for us to travel quickly—on skis. I realise that you may not have——"

"You forget that I spent many years of my life in this

area before the war," I told him. "I'm quite at home on skis. A little rusty, perhaps, but you need not worry on that score.'

"Excellent." He was obviously relieved. "Then it is settled. I shall come for you a little after five o'clock. It will be dark then and I will bring everything that is necessary. Tonight we shall learn if your mission is to stand any chance of success."

It was snowing thickly by the time we left the outskirts of Hayanger and moved north. During the afternoon, according to Tvedt, the Germans had begun a house-to-house search, but it had been impossible to say whether this had been merely a routine matter, or whether they had any definite suspicions. The route we were taking was familiar and the shapes of the rocks and mountains, even the tall, rearing pines on either side of the steep ascent had the characteristics of well-remembered landmarks.

I quickly got back into the way of handling skis and Svenson too, proved to be extremely competent. At first, we made good progress and the pack which I carried on my back had been light, but it was gradually becoming heavier and more cumbersome, more clumsy with each passing second. But still I kept on, doggedly determined to maintain pace and speed with the others. In the past, it had been my policy never to concede a point unless compelled to do so by absolute force of citcumstance.

Ascending with skis was a tiring process at the best of times, but now, in almost pitch blackness, with an icy wind keening down the slope, tugging at my clothing, with the flakes of snow swirling in my face, it was a nightmare journey. Fortunately, the covering of snow, piled high into deep drifts in places by the wind, showed up every detail of the surrounding terrain and I knew there would be little difficulty is ski-ing down the further slope once we arrived at the top. The snow covering, inches deep, bore shallow depressions of other ski marks. Germans troops, I thought tightly. Even at that moment, there might be some of them crouched among the dense forests around us, fingers curling tightly on rifle triggers, eyes peering through telescopic sights, following up our movements, choosing their own time in which to shoot us all.

We rested for a few moments at the top of the slope, then launched curselves down the smooth, snow-covered slope beyond, Tvedt in the lead. There was something vaguely exhilarating in that swift descent, in the rush of wind past my face, whipping my clothing back; in the effortless motion which carried me swiftly after the others. Then the bulk of the mountain was behind us and we were gliding silently through tall, sky-rearing trees, along a narrow trail which Tvedt seemed to know like the back of his hand. The wind was a loud, singing noise in my ears, it was difficult to draw a breath. Then we had burst out of the forest, were now in the open once more and I could just make out, in the far distance, halfway up the further slope, the dark speck of a chalet, crouched beneath a patch of pines.

Unerringly, Tvedt led us towards it. No lights showed in the windows and there was no sign that it was, or had been, inhabited. Until we came within twenty yards of it. Then two dark figures rose up out of the snow, rifles in their hands, rifles which were pointed directly at us as we approached.

Aasmund called something in a harsh voice. It was impossible for me to make out the words, which were whipped from his mouth by the lashing wind, but the two men relaxed and lowered their rifles. Leaving our skis outside the chalet, we went inside. There were ten men inside, grim, efficient-looking men who eyed Svenson and myself suspiciously. Svenson nodded to one or two whom he recognised, the others watched us in a sullen silence, still apparently unsure of us. It was not going to be easy to sell the idea of a unified Resistance Movement in the area to men such as these, I thought tightly.

"These men are the leaders of the main groups in this area," explained Tvedt quietly, taking me by the arm and introducing me to them. "Together, they represent close on three hundred men, all sworn to fight the Germans to the last man. But, as you have pointed out, they are lacking in co-operation. We are hoping you can provide that missing ingredient."

"I'll do my best." I said tensely. There was something in the level stares of these men that was oddly disquieting.

"Do you know the Germans from first-hand experience?" asked one of them, a burly, blond-haired man named Collett. "Do you know what they are like, their treachery? Have you had anything to do with the Gestapo?"

"A little." I said quietly. "But that is surely beside the point. The reason I am here is not to tell you how to face the tortures of the Gestapo, nor how to save those of your people taken hostage by the Germans." I was aware that the others were watching me closely now, that I had their undivided attention. "But it must have become increasingly obvious to most of you that if you are to do the most damage to the enemy, then every action must be planned as a military operation; and how many of you are soldiers in the real sense of the word?" No one spoke and I went on quickly, clinching the point, driving home my advantage. "None of you. I thought so. I'll admit that by blowing up an important stretch of railway line, or destroying a bridge, you're hitting at the enemy, but these are mere flea-bites compared with what you can do."

"Perhaps you aren't aware that our activities during the past four months have forced the Germans to bring in an extra division of men," said Collett fiercely. "You cannot say that this is a flea-bite. With the war as it is, they need every division they can get on other fronts. If we can continue to tie their men up here, away from the fighting front, then I consider that we've performed something of real military importance."

I nodded. "I wasn't aware of that." I admitted. "But

you can still do more. Believe me, I'm not here to order you to do anything. All I can do is advise. I've no wish to take over command from any of you. You know your men and you know this country. But isolated incidents are merely scratching at the surface. We need explosives, more than can be landed here by British submarines."

"And where do you propose that we should get them?" demanded Sedensvey, small and slight, but with a cruel, hungry look in his deep-set eyes.

"From the Germans." I said, smiling grimly. "With a fresh division in the area, it ought to be possible to waylay some of their supply lorries and help ourselves, particularly if we combine such an operation with an attack on their forces in the town. Have they any tank forces in the area?"

The men looked at each other and it was a few moments before anyone spoke, then Collett said hoarsely: "We've seen one or two tanks during the past few days, but surely you aren't suggesting we should capture any of them?"

"Not capture them, destroy them. A handful of grenades in the right place ought to be sufficient to knock out a tank. At least it will give them something to think about and keep them occupied while we carry out the major operation. Especially, if we attack in broad daylight."

"In daylight!" There were murmurs of astonishment. "But that's simply asking for trouble."

"Perhaps. But we would, at least, have the advantage of surprise. They would never expect it. In broad daylight, in the main streets of the town, they must imagine themselves to be secure. The overlords, impervious to attack."

"My God, but the idea appeals to me," said Tvedt in a loud voice. "It's a long time since anyone put forward an idea like that." He clapped me on the shoulder. "And if we get our hands on some high explosive at the same time, I vote we should listen to his plans and then decide. How many men would we need for your plan?"

"For the attack in the streets, very few. Not more than ten. Too many and it will be impossible for the vast majority of them to get away, whereas a small handful could make their get-away relatively easily in the ensuing commotion."

"And for the other part of the operation?"

"That's a different proposition altogether. We'll have to work that out in detail, but the more men we can get together, the better. They'll have any convoy heavily guarded."

"That makes sense," agreed Collett grudgingly. "I agree, in principle with your plan."

I watched the other carefully, but Collett did not change the expression on his face. The expression was one of cool, thoughtful reserve. There was no doubt that he had got to be leader of his own particular group by sheer strength of character and also because he was, by sheer habit, a cautious and careful man. I knew what he was thinking inwardly, the same thing that had struck all of the others. For those in the town, the small group, there would be danger, but the chances of getting away without suffering casualties, were reasonably high. But for the larger group, attacking the convoy, there would inevitably be many casualties. That the enemy might be expecting an attack on the convoy, was foreseen by everyone concerned.

But like the others, too, his mind had not yet grasped fully the implications of the situation. He was only able, at present, to take the short-term view, and that view was not particularly encouraging.

"There will be men killed, of course," he said finally, some of the grimness melting from his features. "That will be inevitably, undeniably so."

"Yes." I said thoughtfully. "That's true, I'm afraid."

The other pursued his inner thoughts for a while, dragging his teeth absently over his lover lip. Inwardly, I wondered whether he was now beginning to regret his earlier decision to agree with the plan. It was possible that the more he thought about it, the less agreeable he might be.

Abruptly, I said: "It's imperative that we take the decision now. Are you with me in this plan. We can hit the enemy and hit them hard, but I shall need the co-operation of everyone, yourselves and the men under your command."

Two minutes later, after talking tersely among themselves, they gave their answer. They were ready to put the plan into operation.

Chapter Three

The Night Intruders

IT might have been bearable without the wind. I moved heavily behind the window, peering out along the street. The sun was low even though it was only an hour after midday and there were still several people in the street. The wind picked at the loose snow on the ledge of the window and whirled it away in tiny gusts, but always, there seemed to be more to take its place, although it had stopped snowing two days earlier. I sat up slowly, pulling my coat more tightly around me. There was no warmth in the sunlight which came through the window and traced a pattern of light and shadow on the floor of the room.

That particular house had been carefully chosen, for several reasons. It overlooked a particularly busy intersection and had been thoroughly searched by a German patrol only three hours earlier. They had left, satisfied, and it was highly unlikely that they would be back for another two days at least.

Tvedt, smoking an ersatz cigarette, drew on it deeply, sucking in his pale cheeks so that the hollows emphasised the tightness of his mouth and the overhanging bushiness of his thick brows. His eyes were scowling as he stared moodily out of the window, occasionally blinking his eyes against the strong sunlight.

"How much longer before they come?" he said hoarsely, shifting his position slightly. "Surely it must be time."

I glanced at my watch, remembered with a slight sense of irritation that I had checked it barely twenty seconds before. "Another fifteen minutes at least, if they're on time." Somehow or other, I managed to keep the tremor out of my voice. "Stop worrying. It's the others who have all of the worrying to do. I only hope to God that everything goes all right with them."

"Collett knows what he's doing. He's a good man and he knows the Germans. If I know him, he'll have his men in position an hour before that convoy is due to reach the forest. Don't worry about him." He stared down at the cigarette, seemingly obvious of the smoke which laced painfully across his eyes. "I've got a feeling that something is going to go wrong. If not with them, then with us." Shuffling to his feet, he moved forward, keeping his head down, throwing a swift glance towards the window on the opposite side of the street. Three other men were in that room, directly opposite us. Down below, in the room immediately below us, two others were ready with the grenades. They would be in the most danger initially. The street was full of German soldiers, walking in pairs or small groups, some attempting to fraternise with the girls on the pavements. It was a sunny day in late winter and they would have been less than human, I thought, if they could have resisted talking with a pretty girl.

Almost three weeks had passed since that night among the pines on the lonely mountain side outside Hayanger when I had meet the leaders of the individual resistance units for the first time. During those three weeks, a lot had happened. It had not been easy to get agreement from everyone. There were the usual dissenters even among those men who spoke of deeds against the enemy, who claimed that carrying the battle to the German forces in Norway was the only aim they now had in life, and that nothing else mattered so long as they killed Germans and destroyed their equipment.

But gradually, diplomatically, most of these proud, fierce men had seen my particular point of view and had thrown in their lot with the others. We had held secret meetings in the forests and several times in a large cave in the mountains which I had known myself, from my early years there. The Germans in Hayanger were undoubtedly suspicious and as we later learned, the submarine had been sighted leaving the fiord, but the surface vessels had lost it in the darkness.

It was with a feeling of contented satisfaction that I looked back over the days just past. In the beginning, it had seemed an impossible task, to weld these individual—in many cases, isolated—units into a coherent whole, to drill into them the precise, military way to plan an operation. I had been pleasantly surprised at the weapons they had managed to hide away during the dark days when the enemy had first occupied their country. Very few of the population had handed in their guns as they had been ordered to by the enemy. Added to those which had been captured by the patriots during past guerilla attacks, they came to quite a sizeable total, something to be reckoned with, when it came to planning something such as this.

"Less than ten minutes now," said Svenson tightly. There was a faint quaver to his voice, one which he desperately tried to hide. The statement brought my mind back to the here and now with a mental jolt.

A ghost of a smiled hovered on Svenson's thin lips. He moved a little closer to the window, fingering the barrel of his automatic weapon. There was something almost animal-like in the expression on his face. Around his temples, where the hair was already turning grey, the sunlight glinted briefly on his scalp and I noticed that, in spite of the coldness inside the room, there was a thin film of perspiration on his skin.

Carefully, I inserted a fresh magazine into my own weapon, checked it swiftly. I could feel the tension beginning to tie the muscles of my stomach into hard knots. Ten minutes and then two action-filled minutes in which a thousand things could go wrong. For me, the personal disaster would be greater than for any of the others. This had been my idea from the very beginning. If I was to continue with the work which had been allotted to me, it was essential that nothing should go wrong.

"There seem to be more soldiers around than usual," remarked Tvedt thinly. He had raised himself slightly until his eyes were on a level with the edge of the window. "Do you think they could have got wind of what's going to happen?"

I started to shrug, then restrained myself. The gesture seemed too nonchalant. "That's not possible." I said. I lifted my head slightly, glanced down into the street. Was it my imagination, or were there more Germans down there than normal at that time in the early afternoon. It seemed to my wandering gaze that a great many of them carried their rifles slung over their shoulders and I could just make out a larger group of them in the distance, near a corner on the far side of the intersection. Within seven minutes or so, a couple of heavy German tanks were due to rumble down one of those streets and pass along the road directly below our window. It was more of a show of strength on the part of the enemy, a constant reminder to the people of Hayanger that they were an occupied town and that any resistance could be ruthlessly crushed.

For the past eight days, we had timed the approach, checked the route taken by these tanks. There seemed, on the surface of things, to be no reason why anything should be changed in any detail. But knowing the enemy, one could never be absolutely certain. At the last minute, they might decide to alter the time, or send the tanks along another road through the town.

"Is everyone in position?" It seemed a stupid question to ask, but I had the feeling that I had to say something. The seconds were beginning to drag, to stretch themselves out. There was a sensation of uneasy stillness, a continual tension, like a premonition of disaster hanging over everything. However, the men were ready. They had been waiting for most of the morning; a seemingly endless period. If a German patrol had appeared on the scene and begun another house-to-house check, we would all have been lost. Luckily, the sun was shining straight along the street and would temporarily blind the men in the tanks and any soldiers in the vicinity. They would have a difficult time locating us against its glare.

"The men below know what to do when the tanks arrive?" I spoke without turning my head.

It was Svenson who answered: "They'll use their grenades on the first tank. Before the second has a chance to put its nose around the corner. They always move slowly when turning into the main street." He paused, then went on seriously, "but I reckon you've cut things a little fine. Fifteen seconds at the most and then all hell will be let loose."

"That's why we're here." I said tersely. "We take care of every soldier who tries to make trouble—and the second tank too if they manage to get it into position before the men get away."

Slowly, very slowly, I raised my eyes until they were just above the level of the window ledge. Still no sign that any of the soldiers in the street was more suspicious than usual. At the corner, one of them had stopped two men and was examining their papers, the sunlight glinting off the barrel of his rifle. But apart from that, the scene was no different from what we had seen on all of the earlier occasions when we had checked every detail in preparation for today.

"I can hear them coming." Svenson caught my arm. "I'm sure of it."

Nodding, I felt myself swallowing dryly. I felt cold, colder than when I had first come up to this room more than two hours before and in spite of the tight control I had on myself, I know my shoulders and arms were shaking in little spasms, and that there was nothing I could do about it. I glanced down at my hands on the stock of the automatic and flexed my fingers slightly. They moved slowly and jerkily, as though they belonged to someone else.

The rumble of the approaching tanks was clearly audible now, disturbing the stillness of the early afternoon. A thousand thoughts ran through my brain as I crouched there. How many yards between those two tanks? Ten, fifteen? And were there only two of them? What if the German Kommandant had decided to show the people of Hayanger the irresistible might of the German army of occupation? What if there were more? I blinked several times, eased my legs into a more comfortable position and tightened my grip on the gun.

Ten seconds passed, and then fifteen. Then the ugly snout of the first tank pushed itself into view around the corner of the street less than twelve yards away, edged itself around the corner. Even from that distance, it seemed so large, so indestructible, so invulnerable to anything we could use against it. You bloody crazy fool! I thought savagely as I watched it rumble forward; sending two men armed with grenades out to destroy that gargantuan monster of tough steel. I was sending those men to their deaths and because they believed in me, they would go willingly. Oh God, why I had believed it possible to put a tank such as that out of action, it was impossible to understand. But the pundits said that it could be done, that if one could get close enough to it, beneath the trajectory of the solitary machine-gun two grenades were all that would be needed

But had military pundits taken into consideration all of the other facts which were relevant on this particular occasion? The fact that there would be only a few seconds in which to throw those grenades, that there were over a score of armed German soldiers standing around in all directions, and that neither of these two men who had been chosen, had been trained as a soldier.

My tongue seemed to fill my mouth in a puffy lump. With almost a sense of shock, I realised that the tank was in the street, the turret gun swivelling slightly; a ponderous creature of power and strength. It has to succeed, I thought, it has to succeed.

Even though I knew what was coming, the sudden appearance of the two men in the street below, came with the shock of the unexpected. They did not hesitate. The little figures seemed to move with a singleness of purpose that was almost frightening. I felt like cheering out aloud as I saw them reach to within two yards of the tank as it lumbered forward. It was all over in five seconds—literally. The first grenade struck the gun turret and bounced off into the road, but the second flew straight and true through the vizor. The explosion, when it came, seemed oddly muffled. There was a faint puff of black, oily smoke from the vizor and then the turret hatch flew open and more smoke boiled out.

Then a second explosion shook the tank and there was a burst of orange flame as either the petrol tank or ammunition detonated. The tank seemed to come apart at the seams. A hand and arm appeared briefly through the open turret hatch as one member of the crew tried desperately, despairingly to pull himself out. Then flames licked up savagely around him and the arm disappeared.

"Watch those troops," I said loudly. The smoke from the burning tank was beginning to fill the street, filtering in through the open window. Down below, the two men were running along the far pavement as a group of German soldiers, reacting swiftly to the situation, began firing after them.

Svenson opened fire savagely, cradling the gun in his arms, squinting along the sights. Two of the German soldiers threw up their arms and collapsed into the gutter as the stream of slugs tore into them. The others turned their heads wildly in an attempt to see where the fire was originating. Out of the corner of my eye, I looked at Tvedt. His lips were curled back over his teeth, his breath coming in uneven, rather hurried gasps and his eyes were slitted, not against the sunlight streaming into the room, but almost in an attitude of pleasure.

By now, there was panic in the street. Where there had been only the burning tank and two running civilians as the centre of attraction, there were men and women in the street and on the pavements, milling around in an attempt to get out of the way of the flying bullets. The German soldiers were firing wildly now, not caring who they hit. As far as they were concerned, the perpetrators of this outrage were Norwegians, and any Norwegians in the vicinity must suffer for it.

Tightening my lips, I lifted the automatic weapon, rested it on the edge of the window, waited until a small group of the enemy had drifted into the sights, and then squeezed the trigger, keeping my finger bar-straight across it, moving the weapon very gently from side to side. Three women had thrown themselves face-downwards on the pavement on the far side of the street and I deliberately aimed over their prone bodies. Behind them, five German soldiers, led by a Sergeant, ran straight into that belting lane of fire, paused for a moment, still upright, clutching at their riven chests and bellies where the bullets had stitched themselves into their tunics, slicing into their quivering flesh.

This was how I had learned to fight and there was a rising exultation within me, bubbling to the surface. I fired burst after burst, into another, larger group of the enemy who came running around the corner to see what the trouble was. Several of them staggered and fell forward on to their faces close to the blazing tank. By now, there was no sign of the two men who had destroyed it, and I guessed that they had made good their get-away. One of the German soldiers who had been hit in the stomach, sat within three feet of the tank, his head thrown back and his mouth open, uttering scream after scream, in a thin, high-pitched voice which grated on my nerves. Lowering the weapon slightly, I fired a long burst into his body, cutting off the scream by a spurt of bullets. For an instant, his hands weaved blindly in front of his face, then he fell back and lay still.

The second tank lumbered cautiously into view and I

saw Svenson leaning half out of the window, thrusting a fresh magazine into his gun, aiming it at the men running alongside the tank. Savagely, I pulled him back into the room, cursing loudly.

"We've got to get out of here," I snapped thickly. "They'll have spotted this window by now and within a few minutes they'll have half a brigade surrounding the house. Come on and hurry!"

For a moment, I thought he was going to refuse, that the mere act of killing the enemy like this had overruled his natural caution. Then he pulled himself together. Slowly, the mad lust for killing seemed to leave him and he got unsteadily to his feet and followed Tvedt and I out of the room, down the narrow stairs and through the door at the back of the building. A fusillade of shoots crashed in the near distance as we ran over the hard soil of the gardens at the rear of the houses. We had planned our escape route several days earlier and every man knew exactly what to do. The weapons were hidden beneath the floor of a cellar in a house some fifty yards from the scene. Then we mingled with the crowds. There would undoubtedly be reprisals for this day's work, I thought wearily. The enemy could not allow an attack such as this, in broad daylight, to go unpunished. I felt a little guilty about what might happen to a lot of innocent men and women because of that we had just done. But in war, I told myself, there was always someone getting hurt and it was essential that acts of sabotage such as this should be continued against the enemy.

"But dammit all, that's impossible." I said harshly, staring across at Collett. Six hours had passed since the successful attack in Hayanger and we were once again in the wooden chalet on the mountain slope outside the town. "You must have been mistaken."

"There was no possible mistake," repeated the other fiercely. "I say that the German troops guarding that convoy knew we were going to attack. What's more to the point, they knew almost to the yard where we were going to hit them. I tell you we have a traitor somewhere among us, someone in league with the enemy, giving them our plans in advance."

I paced up and down the room for several moments. It was hard to believe that what the other claimed could possibly be true. Yet on the face of it, it seemed to be the only possible explanation for what had happened. I seated myself at the table again, opposite the other. "Perhaps you had better explain things from the beginning again, if you don't mind." I said wearily, running the back of my hand over my forehead. It was throbbing painfully.

"There's very little to explain," growled the other. "We were in position almost half an hour before the convoy was due to arrive at that point. Every single man knew exactly what to do. There could be no mistake—or so we thought. But when the convoy finally arrived——" He paused deliberately, for effect, then went on heavily: "The guard had been doubled and at least five of the trucks carried machine-guns. It was massacre, there's no other word to describe it."

"But you managed to get the explosive." I said dully. Now, it seemed such a hollow victory.

He nodded his head slowly. "We got the explosive. But we lost twenty-eight men in the process. *Twenty-eight men*." He stressed the words harshly. "I anticipated casualties. They were inevitable in an operation of this magnitude. But as many as that." He rose heavily to his feet and spread his hands in front of him in a gesture full of meaning.

"And you feel certain that you were betrayed?" Svenson butted in, watching the other closely.

"Yes. I'm positive." Collett glared at him as though expecting the other to argue the point with him.

"Then this is more serious than I had thought." Feeling suddenly weary, I slumped down in the chair and rested my head on my hands. If the traitor were among the men in the movement, and at the moment that seemed to only possible assumption to make, it would be like looking for a needle in a haystack. The only thing we did know for certain, was that it was unlikely that the man who had betrayed the others would have been in that group, otherwise he would have risked either being killed himself, or he would have made himself conspicuous by his actions during the fighting.

I tried to cast my mind over the names and actions of the men who had been with me that afternoon, but none of them seemed likely candidates for this role.

"Well, what do you think we ought to do about it?" persisted Collett, forcing his point home.

"There's very little we can do at the moment." I told him harshly. "You don't expect the guilty person to give himself up to us, do you? We can only keep our eyes open. Sooner or later, he's going to give himself away."

"And how many more good men are we going to lose before that happens?"

"Oh for God's sake, how should I know," I snapped irritably. The other's fears were justified, I knew, but his constant harping on the subject was eating at my nerves, which were already stretched almost to breaking point. I had come to the chalet expecting to hear that the attack on the German convoy had enjoyed the same kind of success as our own, smaller and less spectacular venture; and now this had happened. Strictly speaking, rooting out a traitor among the ranks was none of my business. These men knew each other intimately, knew who could be trusted implicitly and who couldn't, could watch each other for anything suspicious. But, in a way, I felt responsible. This had been my plan from the beginning. And although, theoretically, there was nothing with which I could reproach myself, nothing for which I would ever have to answer to any military court; I knew that I had to face up to my most demanding and insistent critic—my own conscience.

That night, the explosive was taken from the chalet

where it had been temporarily stored and hidden in the bleak cave high on the mountain slope. It was beginning to snow a little when we made our way back to the chalet from the cave a little before four o' clock in the morning although there were a few breaks in the cloud low down on the horizon and a single star shone brilliantly, frostily clear, just above the trees. With our automatic carbines strapped across our shoulders, we made good progress down the smooth, steep slopes, winding our way skilfully in and out of the tall trees. The chalet, perched on the slope, looked deserted as we glided up to it, soundless on the skis.

Slowly and carefully, we made our way inside. The three men there, in the solitary room, glanced up as we entered. The man beside the window lowered his rifle and gave us a tight grin.

"There's coffee ready," he said, jerking his thumb in the direction of the fire. "It's still hot."

I drank the sour liquid slowly, feeling it bringing some of the warmth back into my chilled body. There was no sugar available, that being one of the many luxuries which the Norwegian people had to do without, unless they had means of getting it from the Germans in exchange for valuable information.

"Was there any trouble?" asked Collett thickly. He sat in the corner, checking the mechanism of his rifle methodically.

"None." I said. "Everything is safely hidden. We may be able to use some of that explosive very soon. But for the time being, we'll have to be careful. The Germans know now that there's a very big group of patriots working in this area and they'll be on their guard. Even with the men we have available, their troops still outnumber us by more than ten-to-one." I drained the mug, set it down on the wooden table. "Any word yet from Hayanger? About any hostages being taken, I mean."

"They've made no move so far," growled Collett. He slid the bolt of his carbine sharply into place, then stood up; a huge man, towering over the others. "But if they do, there's very little we can do about it. They've shot a lot of men and women in other towns. Now that we've shown our hand, it's only to be expected that they'll do the same here. Anyone they suspect of co-operating with us will be arrested by the Gestapo and taken away for questioning. And I'm sure that everyone here knows exactly what that means." His words fell into a muffling silence.

"We knew that might happen when we started this," I told him fiercely. "Now I think the best thing we can do at the moment is go back to——"

"Quiet!" Tvedt hissed the sudden warning in a sharp voice, a mere exhalation that was, however, sufficient to bring silence into the room. Swiftly, noiselessly, I moved over to the window in answer to his urgent signal. Crouching down against the horizontal logs which made up the chalet wall, I knelt close beside him, ears straining to pick up the faintest sound.

"I'm sure I heard something out there," he said thinly, lips close to my ear. "I couldn't say what it was, but I'm certain that it wasn't any of the others. They should all be home by now."

"Put that fire out—quickly!" I snapped. Barely had I spoken than Tvedt had moved to the hearth, pouring the dregs from the coffee pot on to the glowing embers. There was a faint hiss and then the room was in total darkness, the lamp on the table extinguished instantly as Collett moved forward, cat-like and silent.

Cautiously, I drew aside the wooden shutters on the window, lifted my head and peered out into the snowy darkness. The trees near at hand were tall, rearing columns of dark shadow, silhouetted against the background of snow. To one side, the mountain rose up towards the black, cloud-laden sky, the peaks standing out starkly against the night. At first, I could see nothing. There was no movement on the snow and even when I refocused my eyes to take in details closer at hand, among the trees themselves, I could see nothing. I was vaguely aware of

Collett, pressing against me, shaggy head lifted as he squinted out into the night. Then I heard him draw in a quick breath. Grasping my arm, he said urgently. "There. Just below the skyline to the right. About a dozen of them. German ski-troops!"

Swiftly, I turned my head, glanced in the direction he had indicated and saw them at once, gliding down from the ridge which overlooked the broad, shallow valley. In the distance, they were little more than tiny, black dots, coming closer with every second. Even as I watched, there was the shrill blast of a high-pitched whistle and the whole line seemed to shift direction slightly. Where they had originally been heading straight down the snow-covered slope, in the direction of the floor of the valley, they had now curved round a little and I saw, with a little thrill of alarm, that they were heading straight for the chalet, that if they held their present direction, they would hit the bottom of the valley and then glide upward, carried smoothly by their own momentum, until they reached us. There was little time in which to act.

"They know that we're here," I snapped thinly. "Somehow, I doubt whether this is just another routine check."

"How many are there?" grunted one of the men in the background. His voice was a harsh whisper of sound.

"About a dozen, possibly fifteen," I said. "We may be able to hold them off, but if they bring up any more—and God alone knows how many may be scouring the mountains for us at this moment, we'll be finished before morning."

"What do we do? Stay and fight, or try to get away while we still have the chance." Collett shifted his huge bulk quickly, lithely away from the window, slipped off the safety catch of his weapon. There was something almost tigerish in the way he moved, shoulders hunched forward a little, head thrust upright on his thick neck. He gripped the weapon tightly in his huge, gnarled hands and his eyes were bright in the shadow of his face.

I thought swiftly. The enemy troops would be upon us within a couple of minutes, I reasoned. If they thought we were still there, in the chalet, they might pause before they attacked. The mere fact that the person in charge had used that whistle to direct his men, was sufficient proof that they did not really expect to take us completely by surprise. No, I reflected, they were quite prepared to surround the chalet and either fight it out there and then, or keep us there until they brought up more reinforcements.

"We'd never stand a chance trying to get away down the slope," grunted Tvedt. "And they would shoot us down before we had gone a quarter of a mile if we tried to get away up the slope to the rear. I vote that we stay here and fight it out with them. There's only the cover of the trees out there and to rush the chalet, they'll be forced to cross that patch of open ground and we can pick them off easily."

"Aye." Collett nodded his head quickly. "If we're to die, at least we can take most of them with us."

"That will solve nothing," I told him pointedly. My mind was racing, assessing all probabilities and possibilities, rejecting one scheme after another. If two or three of us could draw them off, the others could get away."

"But those men out there are seasoned ski-troops," protested Tvedt. "They've been trained for this type of work. Would any of us stand a chance of survival, trying to draw them off."

"We might," I reached a quick decision. "It will all depend on how many of them decide to follow us. If they all come after us, we'll have to rely on throwing them off our trail among the trees on the far slope. If only half of them come, then those remaining behind, ought be able to take care of them."

I rose swiftly to my feet. "There's no time to be lost. I want Tvedt and Svenson to come with me. The others stay here. If any of them head for the chalet, I want you to take care of them all. It may well be that we won't be able to use this place after tonight, so it's important that all of the other members should be alerted."

There were no murmurs of dissent and less than thirty seconds later, Tvedt and Svenson followed me out of the chalet, rifles across our backs and pistols stuffed inside our belts. It was the work of a few moments to slip on the skis and then we were moving swiftly down the side of the mountain, weaving expertly in and out of the trees. Bursting out into the open, we plunged down the slope at breakneck speed, thrusting ourselves forward with the ski-ing sticks to gain the maximum speed.

Out of the corner of my vision, with the wind whipping tears into my eyes, I caught a blurred impression of the German troops moving down on us from the right in a long line. For a moment, I thought that they had failed to see us; then there was the shrill blast of a whistle once more, a sound that was repeated three times and the outer half of that moving line of men suddenly wheeled and began to plunge down the slope after us in a flurry of snow.

So far, so good, I thought savagely. Now to lead them away from the chalet. Speeding down the slope, with the bitter wind blowing right through me, lashing my face, I nevertheless felt a small but undeniable response to the challenge now facing us which left me a little heady and exhilarated. Over my shoulder, I saw that we were still maintaining the distance between us, that we would remain ahead of the enemy, at least until we reached the top of the far slope. There was little point in heading back to Hayanger. That would have been the height of foolishness. We had to lure these men into the snow-covered wilderness which lay to the east and kill them there.

Svenson and Tvedt were now ten or twenty yards away. They had spread out, so that we were reasonably widely separated, making more difficult targets should any of the enemy, moving up from behind, open fire in the hope of hitting one of us with a lucky shot. I reached the top of the ridge, paused for a moment, looking behind me. The enemy were still there, closely bunched together, closing in for the kill.

Five of them, I counted. Better than we had hoped for. Pulling the pistol from my belt, I fired swiftly at the line of advancing men. Three shots and one of the men suddenly slithered forward on to his face, his momentum carrying him forward a couple of yards before he stopped. The others still came on, relentlessly.

Waving my arm, I motioned Tvedt and Svenson to keep moving. There was no cover here. A few bare rocks which thrust themselves up out of the snow, but no trees. I paused for a moment longer, then pushed myself off with the ski-ing sticks, gathering speed as I fled down the slope. Behind me, came the four German soldiers, now determined to avenge the death of their companion.

On the far slope, which rose up in front of us, perhaps half a mile away, there was a thick clump of trees which would afford us excellent cover if only we could make it there. For a long moment, I thought we had a good chance of reaching it before the enemy caught up with us, but that hope was dashed, died almost before it was born, as I looked behind me and saw the four Germans, handling their skis skilfully, spreading out slightly to take advantage of the terrain, and to attack us from both flanks. They were narrowing the distance rapidly and it was inevitable that they would catch us long before we reached the trees.

There was only one thing to do now, I thought savagely, and it had to be done without hesitation if we were to save ourselves. Aware that Tvedt and Svenson were watching me closely, I signalled to them to stop at the bottom of the slope. Five seconds later, twisting my skis sharply, I came to an abrupt halt in a flurry of powdery snow. Desperately, I pulled the pistol from my belt, lying flat in the snow. The move had taken the enemy completely by surprise. They had been so certain that we would continue on and head for the trees that they were unable to stop themselves in time. Briefly, I saw the leader coming straight for me down the slope, trying desperately to halt his headlong plunge. But even as he turned the skis I brought up the pistol and fired at almost point-blank range. Snow from his skis half blinded me and a moment later, his inert body crashed into mine as he tumbled headlong down the slope.

Savagely, I fought to extricate myself, thrusting his dead weight off my arms and shoulders. It was impossible to tell at that moment, whether he was dead or alive, whether or not my bullet had found its mark. For a moment, there was panic in my brain, a panic which seemed to give me superhuman strength. Heaving him away from me, I glanced at his face, saw that my bullet had taken him cleanly through the head, killing him instantly.

The shuddering impact of his body hitting mine had knocked the pistol from my grasp and it was now lying somewhere in the snow. I knew there was no time for me to find it before the others were upon me and as my brain took over command of my body, I unslung the rifle from around my shoulders, sitting in the snow. Glancing up, I saw that Svenson had wounded one of the enemy, but that the other two were closing in rapidly. One of them was heading directly towards Tvedt as he fired rapidly at the man, blazing away with his pistol. The fourth man was coming rapidly down the slope towards me.

Some part of my mind told me that I could not possibly hope to unsling the rifle and open fire before the other reached me. There was no mistaking the German's intention. He still carried his rifle over his shoulders, his body bent low over his skis, his arms moving like pistons as he used the ski-ing sticks to give him added speed. And yet he had perfect control over the skis, would be able to alter course swiftly and instantly if I tried to roll out of the way and with the skis still strapped to my own feet, it would be a clumsy attempt to escape at best.

I could almost see the other's face, brutal and savage, filled with a determined lust to kill, knowing that he had me at his mercy. Somehow, I got the rifle from my shoulder, tried to swing the cumbersome weight around, my finger on the trigger. Desperately, I lifted the barrel, squeezed the trigger, trying to throw myself to one side in the same movement. The trigger did not move. Madly, I pressed it again, then cursed myself for not remembering to take off the safety catch. The German soldier was less than ten yards away now, skis making a faint swishing sound on the snow. My mind was numb, my brain working with difficulty. Death was only a few seconds away and I seemed unable to do anything about it.

I could feel my heart going very fast and for some odd reason, those few seconds seemed to be dragged out into an interminable nightmare. Fumbling, I managed to slip off the safety catch of the rifle, but even at that moment, I knew I would be too late. Automatically, galvanising my legs into sudden action, I thrust myself sideways. There was snow in my mouth and eyes, and a roaring in my ears which threatened to drown out every other sound in the world.

Then, incredibly, the German soldier suddenly threw up his arms as if to clutch at something invisible in the sky just above his head. The shining steel of the skis swished past my legs scant inches away. Moments later, as I got unsteadily to my feet, aware of the trembling in my arms and legs, I noticed the half of a ski-ing stick protruding from between the German's shoulder blades. I stood looking down at him for a long moment, my fumbling, dazed mind still scarcely able to comprehend what had happened.

Svenson came up to me. "It was the only thing I could do," he muttered, almost defensively. "I had used up all of the ammunition in the pistol and there was no time to use my rifle."

"Thank God you got him in time," I gasped thiskly. Blood was pounding at the back of my temples and there was a dull, nagging ache behind my eyes. "What about the other two?"

"Both dead," said Tvedt harshly. "That move of yours must have come as a shock to them. They weren't expecting anything like that."

I nodded slowly. "It was the only thing to do. We would have been killed for sure if we'd tried to reach those trees."

There was blood on the snow at my feet, staining the pure white, and the bodies of the dead Germans looked strangely isolated and out of place in the stretching wilderness.

"Do we get rid of the bodies?" asked Svenson, rolling one of the dead men over with his boot. "If we don't they'll be found within hours."

"They'll be missed anyway by dawn," I said slowly. "Besides, there's no time to waste. We have to get back to Hayanger. If Collet and his men do their job properly, no one will be able to connect us with this night's work."

The Germans made no positive move for two days after the attack on their ski patrol. There was no indication that they intended taking any reprisals on any of the townspeople for what had occurred. Occasionally, they made snap searches of houses in the town, obviously looking for arms and explosives, but beyond that, life went on as normal.

But if there were no mass executions, we still had our own worries. Three nights later, in the cellar of the school which was used as a temporary headquarters, Collett broached the subject which had been at the forefront of all our minds for several days. Slowly, deliberately, he leaned forward over the table and crushed out the butt of the ersatz cigarette he had been smoking. The gesture, I thought wearily, guesing what was coming, held an air of decision and finality.

"Let us be perfectly frank, he said harshly. "Somehow, the Germans are getting information about our movements, where we intend to attack, and when. How many men we will use." He held up his right hand as I made to speak. "I know what you're going to say." There was a biting irony in his tone. "That we have no proof of this. But how much more proof do you need? First of all, we lay a trap for that German convoy, only to discover to our cost, that it is the Germans who have laid the trap, knowing our plans beforehand, and we lose a lot of good men. Mere coincidence? Perhaps, but that isn't the end. Three nights ago, a German patrol attacks the chalet. I'm quite sure that all of us who were there must be convinced that they knew exactly where to come—and that there would be some of us there. They were ready for trouble, and looking for it."

He pounded the table with his clenched fist, the gesture insistent in its unrestrained urgency. "We must discover this traitor and deal with him. And when we do find him, I insist that he be shot. Such a man could destroy us all, and everything we stand for. He doesn't deserve to live."

"How do you suggest we go about it, Collett?" I asked heavily.

"I don't know." He sank back into his chair. "It must be someone who knows our plans—that narrows down the search a little. Most of the men know nothing until the time for action. They wouldn't have the opportunity of getting such information through to the Germans. And it wouldn't be anyone who was either in that group which attacked the convoy, or were in the chalet when the enemy attacked. Surely to God there can't be so many suspects when we eliminate those men?"

He paused, looked around the cellar, eyeing each of us in turn. There was something challenging and provoking in his glance. The words, his tone, were a challenge, inviting reply; and yet there seemed very little to say. He was probably right, of course, I told myself. But that didn't make things any easier.

"What about that man of yours, Tvedt, in the Kommandant's kitchens. I know he's been supplying us with a lot of valuable information in the past, but how do we know that he isn't the traitor? He has the most opportunity of passing word back to the Germans."

Tvedt shook his head swiftly and there was something almost savage in his reply. "That's impossible. I'll stake my life on his loyalty."

"Perhaps," growled the other. "But I'm not willing to stake mine without proof. His face hardened. "I'm afraid that you seem to have things a little out of focus here. I agreed to join in this campaign you've planned against the enemy because on the face of it, it seemed the logical thing to do. But I refuse to subject my own life and those of my men to the risk of being caught by the enemy, because you have a man in your ranks who cannot be trusted. Do I have to remind everyone here that this is wartime, that no matter what our Government does, we are still fighting the enemy, that individual feelings, trials and sufferings are of no account at all?"

His words, the bitter tone and the lashing bite behind them, provoked no reaction of any kind from the rest of the men seated around the long, wooden table. I turned my head slowly, to watch their expressions, but for all that there were, their faces might have been carved from granite. As a British soldier, this was not really my affair at all. I was there, merely to advise and to bring to them my knowledge of fighting the enemy.

Collett smiled sardonically to himself, lips curving slightly. "I think I understand," he said throatily. "I don't really think there's more for me to say. If you cannot promise that the traitor among your ranks will be caught and punished, that he will be shot, then I'm afraid I cannot go through with any other plans that you might have in mind."

He pushed back his chair, scraping it loudly on the stone floor and rose slowly to his feet, remaining for a moment with his large hands flat on the table, resting his weight on them.

"What in God's name are you talking about, Collett?" demanded Svenson thickly, angrily. His eyebrows were arched into a furrowed brow. "Do you intend to withdraw from this campaign against the enemy?"

"In a way—yes. I intend to go back and fight the Germans in my own way, as I did before Bjornson arrived here with his high-flown ideas of forcing us all to join together." His glanced whipped round and settled briefly on me. "You mean well," he said condescendingly, "I realise that. But so far, my group had lost almost thirty men and I see that if I remain with you, I shall lose many more in the near future. I have their welfare to consider as well as my own." He paused, as though another thought had struck him, then shrugged. "However, if you have plans for another full-scale attack on the enemy, I may reconsider my decision, provided that it shows a reasonable chance of success and you make every possible effort to trace this man."

Svenson jerked back in his chair, bit his lower lip, then relaxed. "What do you say?" His voice was very soft and quite toneless as he turned to me.

"I did have something in mind," I said slowly. "I was hoping to bring it up at this meeting."

"Out with it then," muttered Collett abruptly. "I'll listen, but that's all I promise at the moment. If it's a worhwhile plan, I may agree to reverse my decision."

"It won't be easy," I eyed the other steadily. "And this time, it's essential that nothing should go wrong." I paused, then went on: "I was thinking about the radar station which the Germans have set up along the coast. Destroying that would set back their defences along the coast several months."

CHAPTER FOUR

The Return

"VERY interesting," said Collett, after I had finished outlining the plan for the blowing-up of the German radar station. "And on quite a large scale too." His voice was dry, sceptical. "Very interesting indeed—and most instructive. Unfortunately, I cannot see how it can possibly succeed. There are almost fifty guards there, the entire area is sealed off and one would have to get through three sepearate layers of barbed wire before you were even inside the perimeter defences. This is a lunatic idea, if I ever heard one. I want no part of it."

I shrugged, keeping my sudden anger under control. "Very well, you need have no part of it. I'm quite certain that we have plenty of men for the task without calling upon your group." Inwardly, I was puzzled over the other's behaviour. There seemed to be something more to his refusal to join us than fear of being betrayed to the Germans. I thought, for one fleeting moment, that perhaps he had wanted to carry out a campaign such as this himself, in order to better himself in the eyes of the rest of the men; and was angry only inasmuch as the idea had been suggested by me. But I dismissed that notion almost instantly. As leader of one of the largest groups of resistance fighters in this part of Norway, he could quite easily have seen to it that he and his men had the lion's share of the attack.

After he had gone, there was silence inside the bare, white-walled room for a long moment. Then Svenson stirerd himself uneasily, coughed nervously and said: "What do you think we ought to do? Perhaps he had a point there, you know. If there is a traitor among us, it's quite feasible that we might all be utterly annihilated once we attack that radar station. Perhaps we should abandon the plan until we're sure."

"No. We'll go ahead as planned." I said sharply. "This is important."

"Are you willing to risk the lives of these men in what might be an abortive attack?" asked Tvedt calmly. He did not look up but continued to stare down at the interlocked fingers of his hands, resting on the table in front of him.

"Suppose we leave that until nearer the time of the attack." I suggested. "For the time being, there are a lot of details which will have to be worked out. Can you spare any men during the next three or four weeks?" I turned to Svenson:

"I'll need them to make checks on the lay-out of that station. Check on the guards, where they have their machine-gun posts located. How many there are. Whether they have any security check on the roads leading to that station and if so, how far out these checks extend. All of this will have to be known before we can work out the final plan. As I mentioned earlier, we must attack on the twenty-seventh."

"Why then?" queried Svenson quietly.

"New moon," I said shortly. "We need absolute darkness. At this time of the year we can't depend on cloudy skies and if there was a moon, we could be spotted before we got inside." I tried to be calm and patient in my manner. "Carrying out an attack of this magnitude is going to be a tricky procedure. We'll need all the help from the elements that we can get."

During the days which followed, the Germans moved

more troops into the area. Collett had carried out his threat of working on his own and for a time, it seemed as though he were determined to sabotage our efforts for the big raid by carrying out small attacks against enemy convoys, destroying two bridges over the railway which, although mere pinpricks as far as the enemy were concerned, had the inevitable effect of tightening enemy security in the area, increasing the number of German patrols scouring the countryside. It only needed one of their ski patrols to stumble upon the cave in the mountains to the north where our precious supply of high explosive was hidden and we would be forced to abandon completely our plans to destroy the radar station. For our own part, small bands of men penetrated as close to the defences of the station as possible. Men armed with high-powered binoculars and cameras, taking pictures of the installations, filming the defences with tele-photo lenses which had been captured from the enemy, or hidden since the days of the German occupation of the country, tucked away carefully against such a time as this. As the days passed, we began to build up a composite picture of the station as seen from the outside. We knew the exact location and strength of the outer defence system. We knew the best way of approach so that we would be able to reach the site even in total darkness with the minimum of noise and the maximum of speed.

But as yet, we knew nothing of what lay inside that ring of defences. Then, two weeks after the plan had been suggested, we had our first real stroke of luck. . .

The man who accompanied Svenson was a stranger to me. A slight man, balding, with close-set eyes that stared at me from behind thick lenses. He seemed nervous, on edge, but tried desperately not to show it.

"This is Peder Vannermeyer," explained Svenson. "He has something important to tell us and I thought I ought to bring him to see you right away."

"Are you sure you weren't followed," I said tightly.

"Quite sure," Carl nodded, grinned slightly. "If anyone

tried to follow us, they will have lost themselves in a maze of side streets by now, believe me."

"And this man—can he be trusted?"

"I'm sure he can. He has information which I think is vital to the success of our plan. He is one of the engineers working in the radar station on the coast. He knows the lay-out so well that it will be the work of a few minutes for him to draw us a detailed plan. Is that not so, Peder?"

"Yes, yes. I can do that for you." The other nodded quickly and his rather prominent adam's apple bobbed up and down nervously in his throat.

"So. This is better than I had hoped. And he's willing to do it?"

"I have no love for the Germans," protested the other quickly in a rush of words. "But I cannot fight like others do. I am no use with a rifle or grenades. But if I can help with——"

"You can," I said grimly. "Sit down at the table and draw out that plan of the radar station and don't forget anything." I still wasn't sure of him. It would have been so easy for the Germans, if they had any hint that we were due to attack the station, to send out a man such as this, to feed us with the wrong information. Apart from strengthening the defences—and as yet there had been no sign of this—they might want to make doubly sure that we would not succeed, and one of the best ways of doing that, would be to allow a plan of the station, containing the wrong information, to be delivered to us by someone claiming to be a friend of the resistance movement.

While the other seated himself at the table and began drawing out the plan, I drew Svenson to one side.

"Where did you pick him up?" I asked in a low voice, so that the other could not overhear. "And how can we be sure that this information he's so willing to give to us is correct?"

"I've known him for some years," whispered the other softly. "He's quite a character, but a good Norwegian. Scared of the Germans, there's no doubt about that and he probably does a little black market on the side, but I'll stake my life that he's loyal. I didn't find out where he was working until yesterday and it was only this afternoon that I managed to run him down. He wasn't too eager at first. He's afraid that his family will suffer if the Germans find out what he's done."

"That's understandable," I admitted. I looked over Svenson's shoulder to where the little man was working industriously at the table. "If this information is the real thing, it's the biggest break we've had so far. He's the one man who can really help us."

Five minutes later, the other looked up. "I've finished," he said quietly. "I've filled in everything on this drawing that I know. There are a few parts of the station which are restricted to German personnel only. I've marked these, but I'm afraid I can give you no information as to what's in them."

I picked up the drawing, scrutinised it carefully, then nodded quickly, satisfied. "You've been a great help," I said gently. "A very great help to us."

"I only wish I could go with you when you attack," he said, and there was a trace of sadness in his voice. "I'm afraid that most of the people in the town have formed their own opinion of me. My wife is shunned by her neightbours because of what I do. I'm working for the Germans, you see. I'm an electrician, I work at the radar station and therefore, I'm an enemy of my country."

For the first time, I understood something of the forces which must have played their part in this man's mind, in his sudden determination to help us, even though by so doing, he could be shot by the Germans.

"You've helped us enough by doing this," I told him. "Now I think you'd better go and forget that you've ever been here or seen any of us. This will be dangerous work and as you say, you have your family to think of."

He nodded his head, still with that look of sadness on his face. "Yes, yes, that is true, I suppose. But so have many of the men who fight with guns and bombs. They have their families too. Perhaps I could do more for my country if I only had the courage and the strength necessary to do it."

"If you had fought with us, you might not have been such a good security risk as far as the Germans are concerned," I said, taking him by the arm and leading him to the door. "And then we might never have had this kind of information. There are many ways of helping us apart from actually fighting the Germans with guns."

"Perhaps you're right." He was not entirely convinced, but he said nothing more as he went out. From the window, I watched him walking down the street in the late afternoon sunlight; a strangely pathetic little man who had perhaps summoned up more personal courage that afternoon than at any other time in his life. Exhaling slowly, I went back to the table and stared down at the pencilled drawing carefully. With this, there was always a chance that our attack might be successful; and if it were, it would mean that, for some time at least, the enemy chain of radar warning stations along the Norwegian coast would be broken.

Since the heavy snow fall during the day, the temperature had risen steadily though slowly throughout the evening; but it had risen only to beguile us for already, long clammy tendrils of fog which bathing Hayanger and the air struck doubly chill as I made my way through the dimness towards the school which was our headquarters. Hurrying across the quadrangle, pulling the collar of my coat more tightly around my neck, I went inside. The others were already there, the leaders of five small groups of men.

"Everything is ready," said Svenson. Tension was in his voice, but none of it showed through on to his face. "The men have all been alerted and we have five trucks ready."

"Then I'm afraid that they'll all have to be cancelled," I said shortly.

Reaction was immediate. "What was that?" demanded Tvedt. "We made the plans for tonight. We can't call it off now. This may be the only chance we'll get. Besides, we have all of the explosive waiting."

"I realise that," I said wearily. "But believe me, we must cancel the plan for tonight. Instead, I want three men and one of the trucks. We'll be going out to the radar site."

Svenson and the others looked at me in the dim light of the hurricane iamp, perplexed and uncomprehending. In the sudden strained silence, it was possible to hear the rumble of a German army vehicle in the distance.

"I suppose you can give us some explanation of why you've decided to call it off," said Tvedt shortly after a brief pause. "After all we are entitled to——"

"I know. Unfortunately, I can't be certain at the moment. But if I am, I promise that you'll be one of the first to know. I want you to come with me—and Svenson. Then, if I'm right, we'll deliver the attack all right, but tomorrow night instead of tonight."

There was a lot of quiet grumbling from the rest of the men and as they left, I could see quite clearly that if I was wrong in my assumption—and it was a long shot I was playing with very little evidence, merely a hunch—my authority over these men, for what it was worth, would soon be less than nil.

The journey out to the Atlantic coast was fraught with danger. Any vehicle out on the roads after dark was liable to be stopped and searched, and if the driver failed to produce the proper papers and authorisations, the Gestapo stepped in with a ruthless efficiency. But the driver, a short, burly man knew the area well and we seemed to lead charmed lives that night. There was no traffic what ever on the roads he chose and the driving rain which had followed close on the heels of the snow, obliterated very nearly everything on either side of the road in a screen of darkness. We drove without lights all of the way, although it was doubtful too, if the enemy had any patrols out in that weather. Skirting the towns and villages, we finally reached a point some two miles from the radar site and it was here that I ordered the driver to stop the truck.

"We'll go the rest of the way on foot," I said tersely.

Svenson looked at me as if I were out of my mind. "In this weather?" he said incredulously. "But they'd never spot us in this rain. We could get to within a quarter of a mile of the perimeter defences without being seen or heard."

"Perhaps. But I'm taking no chances. We walk the rest of the way."

Grumbling, the others obeyed. Here, the rain had not had sufficient time in which to wash away all of the snow and our feet slipped and sank into an ice-cold slush which made walking a hundred times more difficult than normal. By the time we reached a low hill overlooking the distant site, we were soaked to the skin, our clothing hung limply on our bodies, chafing our flesh with every movement, and the muscles of our legs ached as if we had just finished a gruelling cross-country race.

The long, toiling climb up the hill in pitch blackness, feet slipping in mud and slush had strained Svenson's resources to the limit and he sank down into the mud thankfully when I called a halt. I stretched my aching legs and tried to find a little comfort in the pouring rain. This was something I had not bargained for; weather as atrocious as this. Our progress had been necessarily slow and the march had become a treadmill for the last quarter of a mile.

Pausing to get my breath back, I turned to Tvedt. "Did you bring the night glasses with you?"

He nodded his head wearily, unstrapped them from around his neck and handed them over to me. "I'd still like to know why we had to do an incredibly stupid thing like this," he said in an aggrieved tone. "We might have had all of the men here by now, together with the explosives. The Germans would never be expecting an attack on a night such as this."

"I'm afraid that's exactly what they would be doing," I muttered grimly, peering through the glasses into the rain-filled night. "Want to take a look for yourself? I promised you would be one of the first to know."

He hoisted himself up on to his knees and took the glasses from me without a word, pressing them into his eyes and peering in the direction of my pointing finger. For a long moment, he remained quite still, scarcely breathing, not moving a single muscle, then he lowered the glasses and turned his face towards me. It was impossible even to guess at the expression on his features as he blinked the rain out of his eyes. "My God," he said thinly, "how on earth did you know? How could you possibly have guessed?"

"What in God's name is it?" whispered Svenson, leaning forward. I gave him the glasses. "German troops, lying in wait for us along the road down there," I said, indicating the direction. "And they have several machine-guns lined up, waiting to open up on us."

"So they were warned," said Tvedt in a dull, toneless voice. "Collett was right. If we had carried out the attack as we had planned we would never have stood a chance. They would have wiped us out completely, to the last man."

"Exactly," I said grimly. I licked my dry lips, running the tip of my tongue over my teeth. Everything had now crystallised inside my mind. What had earlier been nothing more than a hunch, a wild idea, was now a certainly.

"If you knew this, or even if you only guessed it," said Svenson, lowering the glasses, "it means that you must have some idea who had been betraying us to the Germans."

I nodded. "I know who it is," I said tightly. "And we must get rid of him tomorrow. Before he can contact his

Germans friends again. Because we'll be attacking tomorrow night. Everything will then go ahead as planned."

"But who is it." Svenson stretched his legs to their fullest extent, lips twisted into a grimace of pain as cramp knotted the muscles.

"None other than our talented resistance leader, Collett. I suspected him some time ago. He knew everything about our plans. But towards the end, he wanted out of the deal. I thought at first, he might be getting scared for his own skin, but he had always struck me as a vicious killer, a man who would stop at nothing to gain his own ends. When he refused to come in with us on this attack, and then held out the hope that, if it was something big enough, he might change his mind, my suspicions became something a little stronger than that, but I still couldn't be sure. So I laid this little trap for him. You'll remember that he stayed at the meeting long enough to learn the date of the attack. He couldn't possibly leave without discovering that. And this time, he wasn't going to risk his own life in the attack. So he played it both ways. Learned the date I'd set, and went immediately to tell his German masters."

"Collett!" Svenson shook his head dazedly. "But it doesn't make sense. He's always been so filled with hatred of the Germans. In the past, whenever there's been an attack, he's been in the thick of it. I know from personal experience that he's killed more than a dozen of their troops."

"I'm not disputing that. But something must have happened during the past few months to make him change his allegiance. I think he's a strange man with a curious personality. He craves power more than anything else. Perhaps, seeing the way that the war has been going lately, he's made up his mind that the Allies cannot hope to win, that sooner or later, Hitler will be the master of the world, certainly of Europe and Britain. And he sees himself being on the losing side if he continues to fight the Germans. So he must have taken it into his head to play it safe, to remain ostensibly with the Norwegian patriots while giving information to the Germans. He's a clever and utterly ruthless man. A dangerous man. That's why I wanted you here with me tonight, to see this for yourselves. Because if we're to save a lot more lives, then Collett will have to be killed."

I felt a little surprised at the quietly callous way in which I could pronounce the death sentence of a man I hardly knew. But it was an unpleasant business, something which had to be done, and the sooner, the better. "Do you think you can get him to come into Hayanger tomorrow morning, as soon as possible, without arousing his suspicions?"

Svenson nodded. "I think it can be arranged," he said slowly. "He may be suspicious though, when he learns that we did not go through with the attack. His German friends may even want to speak with him, to ask him why we did not go through with it, as he had told them we would."

"All the more reason why you should get to him first," I said tightly. I got to my feet. "There's nothing more for us to do here. Let's get back to the lorry out of this damned rein."

"What about those Germans down there?" queried Tvedt as we slithered down the steep slope.

"Leave them where they are," I said grimly. "Being out all night in weather like this will make them think twice about doubling the guards tomorrow night. Somehow, I doubt whether they will take so much stock of what their agents tell them after this. They'll be more inclined to check everything first, for themselves." In silence, we trudged back through the blinding rain to the waiting truck.

The following morning, Collett faced us defiantly across the table in the school cellar. Above us, there was the sound of the children taking up their places in the classrooms.

"Did you have any trouble?" I asked, turning to Tvedt.

He shook his head and took up his position near the door. "None at all," he affirmed. "He wanted to know why you wished to see him, but he came quite willingly."

"Perhaps you will tell me what all this means," said Collett harshly. "If you want my men and I to come in on any other hair-brained scheme with you, then I'm afraid that my answer is still the same." He paused, licked his lips, then went on: "And what happened to your brilliant plans last night. I understand that you did not go through with them. Something go wrong at the last minute, or did the men come to their senses and realise that they couldn't possibly go through with this attack and still survive."

"Nothing like that," I said evenly, realising that the other merely wished to provoke me, was attempting to bluster it out. "It was simply that there seemed little sense in going into that station after the German guards had been alerted."

"Alerted." There was no change of expression on his face and I felt a grudging admiration for the way in which he managed to keep his feeling so tightly under control. "So there is a traitor in the organisation. Now perhaps you'll listen to me and agree that I was right."

"Oh yes, I'll agree you were right, Collett." I leaned forward over the table and stared him straight in the eye. "How could you be otherwise?"

"What do you mean by that?" He glanced around at Svenson and Tvedt. "What is this madman raving about now?"

"Come off it, Collett," I said angrily. "We know that you've been betraying your comrades to the Germans. How long this has been going on, we don't know. But of one thing we *are* certain. That you've done your last job for your German masters. This was a trap that I set for you. I deliberately allowed you to know the date on which we planned to attack, then changed it at the last minute. I'm afraid that the German troops waiting for us on the road leading into the site had a long, cold, wet wait last night."

For a moment, I thought he intended to bluff it out, that he would deny the charge against him. Then his lips curled back in a sudden snarl and his hand darted beneath his shirt, closing around the gun which he always carried there. He had it halfway out of its holster, was turning swiftly towards the door when the silenced weapon in Svenson's hand uttered a faint pop. For an instant, the other's arm and legs worked with a feeble machine-like motion as he tried to hold himstlf upright. Then his fingers relaxed around the butt of the gun and it slipped from his grasp on to the floor. The blood-red stain on his shirt began to grow a little as he stared at me with hate-filled eyes, his lips and the corded muscles of his throat working as he tried to get words out through his trembling mouth.

Then his legs gave way under him and he fell to the floor, his head striking the edge of the table with a dull, sickening thud. Svenson walked over and stared down at the body with dispassionate eyes. "I would never have believed it," he said slowly. "Collett—a traitor."

We cleared the outskirts of Hayanger that night without much difficulty and headed along the road which we had taken the previous night, It was pitch black with a strong wind blowing, sending the dark, low clouds scudding across the sky. There was a drizzling rain which had soaked us to the skin within minutes but as far as we were concerned, it was an ideal night for the task we had in hand.

Once we passed a solitary German truck on the road, but the driver must have mistaken us for an army convoy for he never slowed once and after a brief moment of tensed anticipation, I forced myself to relax as the truck bumped over the uneven road which, in places, had been turned into a veritable quagmire by the rain and melting snow.

We drove ahead slowly, carefully now as we neared our destination. By the time we reached a spot some half a mile from the defensive perimeter, the rain had eased off a little and a few stars were beginning to show through scattered breaks in the cloud. The wind still blew from the north, whirling in our faces as we dropped down from the trucks, lifted the weapons and high explosive from the back of the rear vehicle and struggled forward into the icy cold, that bit into our very bones, numbing our limbs. As we went forward into the darkness, I wondered if I had been right in my assumption that the enemy would be convinced that Collett's information had been false, whether they would have called off their watch on the road leading to the site.

But in spite of the coldness in my body, in spite of the tightness of my nerves, stretched almost to breaking point, and the hard knot of fear in the pit of my stomach, in spite of the fact that we were pledged to carry out an attack on what was virtually an impregnable position, I felt more at ease than at any time since that morning when I had stood over Collett's dead body and had known that the die had been cast.

Now I was setting out to do that for which I had been trained. Everything was almost completely instinctive now. My senses were strained to the utmost limit. The little sounds of the night, just audible above the shrieking of the wind, were abnormally clear, jarring on my ears. The darkness which had helped us considerably during the drive there, now hampered our approach. Without the plans which we had been able to draw up over the long weeks of preparation, we might have wandered around in circles, blundering into the dafences.

With an effort, I shook off the growing sense of unreality as I peered about me into the night. There was a deep and clinging silence over everything which pressed down on us from all sides. I found myself checking my watch several times, glancing at it every few seconds, feeling a sudden sense of urgency as the realisation came to me of how quickly the minutes were slipping by.

"There," said Svenson softly, stopping abruptly.

As the rest of the men went to ground, stretched out in a long line, I crawled forward until I lay beside him. In front of us, the barbed wire wound away into the distance. It had been carefully hidden at this spot by several tall bushes and I breathed a prayer of thankfulness that the other had spotted it in time and nobody had blundered blindly into it.

Beyond the wire, some thirty or forty yards away, tall wooden towers stood out clearly against the starlit darkness, where the clouds had drifted away, leaving the sky clear.

"Those are the three forward machine-gun posts," said the other unnecessarily, as he pulled the wire-cutters from his pocket. "Now I only hope to God that Vannermeyer was right when he said there were no warning systems set up here."

Delicately, he snipped the wire in several places. There were no raucous bells ringing and I relaxed abruptly. I could visualise in my mind's eye, the German guards up in those machine-gun towers, crouched down behind their weapons, eyes peering into the blackness all around them; eyes which were now thoroughly accustomed to the night and could pick out the slightest movement. It required only one man to become a little suspicious, to pull out a torch and shine the beam down on to the ground and that would be the end for most of us. At that range, with at least three machine-guns within fifty yards, it would be virtually impossible for the gunners to miss.

A shiver passed through me, then I pulled myself together and wriggled through the hole in the wire. Now, I thought tensely, our troubles were just about to begin. The possibility of using a diversionary attack to draw off some of the defenders had occurred to me, but I had dismissed it as not only impractical with the limited number of men I had at my disposal, but possibly a dangerous ruse under the present circumstances.

It would give our position away to the enemy at a time when silence was what we needed most. The enemy would not be long in putting two and two together if, for no apparent reason, a bunch of men suddenly attacked the defences on the far side of the site. And once alerted, searchlights would sweep the area, discovering us almost at once.

I crawled forward slowly, the bulk of the silenced pistol a reassuring weight in the pocket of my heavy coat. So far, we had merely accomplished the easiest part of our task. Once inside the defences, we would have to be on the alert every single second. The German guards were noted for their acute sense of hearing and vision; and it needed only one man to put a foot wrong, to give us away completely. Once more, I was thankful for the intense cold and the pitch blackness of the night. Probably more than anything else, it kept the German sentries inside their shelters and they merely peered out now and again to assure themselves that nothing was wrong. Besides, this attack had been scheduled for the previous night and most of the men would have stayed up in that terrible weather, soaked to the skin, and all for nothing.

Svenson tugged urgently at my sleeve and motioned me forward. I cursed myself for day-dreaming at a time such as this and followed him quickly. We were almost upon the outer ring of buildings and beyond them, possibly two hundred yards away, the tall masts of the radar station proper loomed up against the frosty stars. These were our primary objective. The men had been briefed on what they were to do once inside and now they went about their individual tasks quietly and efficiently. What happened now would decide, once and for all, whether my trip here, inside enemy-occupied Norway, had been worth while, whether these men had learned anything from me.

Everywhere there seemed to be silence and a complete lack of movement, which came as a distinct shock to me.

I had expected to find a hive of industry here with men patrolling the area continually, possibly with police dogs, even after dark. But there was nothing like that. For all that I could see, the entire establishment could have been utterly deserted.

But that was a surface illusion, I told myself. Inside those buildings. German technicians would be crouched over radarscopes, watching the Atlantic for any British ships which might be in the vicinity, or any R.A.F. bombers flying in this direction. We skirted two large blocks and, as we passed the larger of the two, I distinctly heard the unmistakable hum of a large generator. For some strange reason, the sound seemed to reassure me, to relax my tensed nerves and muscles a little. It was a recognisable sound, something normal.

Acting on the plan of the site which Vannermeyer had drawn for us, we made our way cautiously forward, pausing whenever anything moved around us in the darkness. Our rubber-soled shoes made no sound on the concrete or the narrow grass verge which skirted the winding roadway connecting the various buildings.

Then, abruptly, there was a sudden sound, a commotion to our right; a harsh voice that yelled something in guttural German which I could not catch. It was followed almost instantly by the faint plop of a silenced weapon, but the damage had been done. The enemy had been alerted by that sudden yell of alarm. It was impossible to tell what had happened, whether a group of our men had stumbled upon a sentry, possibly half-asleep and he had been able to shout before he had been shot. Quite suddenly, the advantage of surprise had been lost, had slipped from our grasp.

"Keep them occupied," I yelled harshly in Norwegian, "while the rest of the men lay the charges and set the detonators." It was the only chance we had of carrying out the plan now that our presence there had been discovered.

A sharp burst of gunfire punctuated my words. A group

of Germans, running into view around the corner of one of the buildings, was met by a lashing volley of gunfire which killed over half of their number and sent the rest scurrying for cover. There was a short spell of silence after that, a silence broken by the vicious, phrenetic hammering of one of the machine-guns. Tracer spewed into the darkness a split second before two searchlights snapped into being, bathing the area in brilliant, actinic brightness, making day out of night, leaving very few shadows in which to hide.

Swiftly, I hurled myself towards the doorway of one of the buildings as a vicious burst of fire hammered off the concrete where I had been a few seconds earlier. One of the men who had been following close on my heels gave a sudden loud cry and pitched forward on to his face as the bullets stitched themselves into his body, killing him instantly. My heart was beginning to thump madly inside my chest and the faint tremor was back in my arms and legs. Acting instinctively, I pulled the pistol from my pocket, squinted up at the great flaring face of the nearer of the two searchlights and pulled the trigger twice. The second shot found its mark. There was the sharp tinkle of breaking glass and the searchlight beam went out. From the other side of the wide square, someone else opened up on the second searchlight, as the beam swung across the fronts of the buildings in the distance, finally settling on a small group of men, trying to find shelter behind a low stone wall. A savage burst of machine-gun fired chipped pieces of stone into the air in the brief second that the beam remained in existence. Then that searchlight, too, had been smashed by a couple of well-aimed shots and darkness, denser than before, closed down about us.

In spite of our temporary advantage, it was a dangerous moment. The enemy had a decided superiority in men and fire-power and, if the battle continued for any length of time, I did not doubt that their added superiority in training could count against us, too. It was essential that we should keep them under cover until the charges were ready and the fuses of the detonators lit. Once that was done, we would be able to withdraw.

Easing myself forward, still hugging the shadows of the wall, I reached a small group of men clustered near a low wall. "Where are the Germans now?" I asked in a hoarse whisper.

One of the men pointed. "Most of them are in that building over there. Could be their living quarters. The rest are in the machine-gun towers and thank God that they're firing blind."

"They won't be for long," I said grimly. "They know what we're after and they can't afford to let us succeed. This place is far too important to them. The Kommandant will risk the lives of all of the men under his command rather than have those towers blown up. We can expect some suicidal attacks very soon."

"We're ready for them," said another man hoarsely. "Let them come."

The Germans did not keep us waiting long. They must have realised that every second was precious. Almost without warning, there was a fusillade of rifle fire from the building directly in front of us and under cover of that fire, a large group of the enemy ran out into the open and began to advance swiftly towards us. Firing from the hip as they came, they got to within thirty feet of our position before our return fire had any appreciable effect on their numbers. Then the savage automatic fire began to tell. Any thoughts I had had earlier that the patriots would turn and run at the first sustained enemy attack were soon dispelled. They stood their ground, in spite of the inevitable casualties, and returned the German fire like veterans.

For a while, it was touch-and-go. Then, unable to withstand our withering, murderous fire, the Germans in the centre of the large square, out in the open, broke and ran for cover. I ckecked my watch. Tensely, I wondered what had happened to the men with the high explosive. They had all been briefed on what they had to do once they reached the radar masts. They surely ought to have completed their task by now. I cursed myself for not having gone with them. Then I noticed that less than two minutes had passed since the enemy had been alerted. It seemed an eternity since the first shot had been fired.

The machine-guns in the towers were still firing down upon us, although for the most part the gunners were shooting wildly. Somewhere in the distance, where another group of men had run into trouble, there came the sharp sounds of exploding grenades. We had certainly stirred up a hornet's nest now, I reflected. More German soldiers tried to rush our position, but were driven back by gun-fire and grenades. There was no point in maintaining silence now that we had been discovered.

Everywhere there was almost complete confusion—but there was a definite purpose behind it, the kind of purpose one would expect from tough, seasoned troops. Nowhere was there any sign of panic on the part of the enemy. From the direction of the tall, skeletal towers came a sharp, vicious burst of stuttering gunfire and a second later there was the noise of a heavy truck being started up. I had thoroughly memorised the lay-out of the site from Van-nermeyer's map and, on the face of it, there seemed no reason for a truck to start up there. Surely the Germans did not think they could run us down in the pitch black-ness? my mind reasoned.

Then I saw the purpose of this move and cursed myself savagely for not having considered the possibility before. The powerful headlights blazed out, replacing the light of the searchlights which had been shot out of existence a little while before. Now they were cutting through the darkness in brilliant bands of light. It was only a matter of minutes before those headlights picked up the crouching figures of the men busily laying the high explosive charges.

I waited tensely for another five seconds, then touched Svenson's arm, rose to my feet and started running madly across the square in the direction of the truck, realising thankfully that it was turned away from us, and that we were still in complete darkness behind it. I gripped the pistol tightly in my left hand, and could just make out the sound of the Norwegian pounding along at my back. In a few seconds we had reached the other side of the square, miraculously unhurt. There was only one chance now of putting this truck out of action and this was not a time for finesse.

The two grenades, lobbed while we were still ten yards away, thrown desperately on the run, hit the side of the truck just behind the driver's cab with metallic thuds, distinctly audible to our ears, then bounced off into the darkness. Not pausing to break step, not even hesitating to fling myself down on to my face as instinct, as precise military training urged me to do, I ran on, half-dragging Svenson with me.

We had only split seconds to wait—the timing had been almost perfect. A line of machine-gun bullets chipped stone off the wall above our heads: and then the twin explosions sounded, so loudly that they might almost have been directly under my feet. There was the savage, shrilling whine of shrapnel cutting the air over my head, then a bursting gush of flame near the edge of the square. The Army truck disintegrated rapidly in a wall of flame, the soggy canvas over the chassis smouldering into tattered shreds which were blown away by the wind and scattered in all directions.

"Stay here," I hissed to Svenson. "There are more of them inside this building. I'll try to get them outside. If I succeed, wait until they're all in the open, away from cover, and then use your gun. I doubt if there can be more than a dozen of them."

"I understand." He crouched low against the wall, face in shadow, the barrel of the automatic carbine lined up squarely on the door.

Swiftly, without bothering to conceal myself, I stepped forward, hammered furiously on the door for a few seconds, then yelled loudly, authoritatively in fluent German: "Quickly! Outside! We have them trapped on the far side of the square. They can't get away this time. Hurry—there's no time to lose!"

For a moment there was silence inside the building and I had the sinking feeling that the ruse was not going to work. But with a German voice giving the order, coupled with the obvious fact hard fighting was definitely going on at the far edge of the square and the undeniable fact that no Norwegian patriot in his right mind would walk up to the door and batter imperiously on it like that, swayed their judgment and dispelled any doubt they may have had. They would have been less than human not to fall for it. Seconds later, the door burst open and a dozen or so German soldiers tumbled out on each other's heels, rifles held stiffly in their hands, the flickering orange glow from the burning truck lighting their faces and uniforms with an eerie colour.

Slipping and stumbling a little in their haste, they advanced at a swift trot, then paused. Before they could turn, run back under cover, the sound of their clattering footsteps was caught up and drowned completely in the savage, tearing bark of our weapons as I pressed myself flat against the wall. This was no war as far as the Germans were concerned. Out in the open, unable to run for shelter, they were massacred. Defenceless, stunned and uncomprehending, they staggered blindly in all directions like a set of puppets, limbs jerking horribly, eyes staring in their grotesque faces. Only one remained on his feet, head jerked back, lips thinned into a grimace of agony, eyes turned heavenward as if looking for some form of divine intervention. He had time for a single, short burst from his weapon as his finger jerked on the trigger in the rapid convulsion of death. The bullets spent themselves harmlessly in the air as he toppled backward over the bodies of his slain companions.

The feeling of rising exhilaration, the slow, heart-warming exultation, did not last for long as more enemy guns opened up all around the square, sending great, shuddering echoes beating beneath the clouds and between the tall buildings. What in God's name were those other men up to? I wondered angrily, checking my watch for what seemed the hundredth time that night. They had now had plenty of time in which to set the explosives and set the fuses. Why the devil weren't they back with the rest of us so that we might begin to withdraw?

"Here come the others now," muttered Svenson calmly, almost as if he had been reading my thoughts. "Not before time either. Things are getting a little too hot around here for my liking."

I gave the order to withdraw thankfully and not a minute too soon. By now, the whole site had been alerted and there was the definite danger of the resistance fighters becoming irretrievably engaged in fierce hand-to-hand fighting, making an orderly withdrawal difficult, if not well-nigh impossible.

Snoothly, skilfully, we pulled back. In the near distance, I could make out vague forms that crouched low in an effort to avoid observation and making their way swiftly forward to ring us around from all sides. But I was now back on balance once more, my body tensed, my brain working swiftly and easily, leaping forward to assess the position as it would be several moments in the future. This was something like a game of chess, I thought amusedly; where you had to plan a great many moves ahead and be able to read your opponent's mind to a certain extent, to counter any moves that he might make.

There had been some casualties, I saw, as we reached the stretches of heavy barbed wire, but not as many as I had expected considering the ferocity of the German retaliation. The enemy had been taken initially by surprise; had not anticipated an attack that night.

I waited untill the last man had leapt through the five-foot gap cut in the wire, then hurried on into the cold darkness to join the main body on the slope of the hill. "How long before those fuses burn through?" I asked tightly.

"Another thirty seconds at the most," muttered one of

the men gruffly. "We arranged them in a rough sequence, twenty-second intervals as far as we could judge. The rate of burning of that fuse won't be a constant factor, but it ought to be near enough for our purpose."

"My God, you didn't give us much time to get free," I acknowledged grimly. Turning, I ordered them down to the bottom of the hill. Running in the darkness, feet slipping, we tried to put as much distance between ourselves and the radar station as possible. There had been no reproof in my voice when I had spoken to the other; indeed it had perhaps been a good thing that they had allowed so little time. It meant that the chances of any of the enemy dismantling the fuses and detonators, now that we had pulled out of the area, were correspondingly reduced.

Quickly, I felt my way down the rocky, treacherous slope. All thought was lost abruptly in the knowledge that the seconds were ticking away all too quickly. Around me, in the cold, clear darkness, the others were running madly downhill, leaping dimly seen obscales. As yet, here had been only a few desultory shots fired after us, bullets that had whistled harmlessly over our heads.

The explosions, when they came, were almost an anticlimax. There was scarcely any flame and, although the ground underfoot trembled slightly, it seemed incredible that they could have destroyed the tall towers. I slithered to a halt and stared behind me, screwing up my eyes to make out details of what had happened. Then swiftly, and in a strange unanimity of silence, the rest of the men paused in their headlong flight and stared at the radar towers, now clearly visible against the background of bright, foaming stars. For one wild, anguished moment, it seemed that they were unharmed, that nothing could possibly harm those gigantic, spiderwork monsters of tough steel. They must surely be indestructible. Then, before our eyes, they began to tilt crazily. It was as if a hand had picked them up several feet, holding them steady in mid-air for a long moment, before releasing its hold and allowing them to fall back on to the ground, tipping them sideways in the process. They began to disintegrate in the air as they came down, metal folding over metal, bars and struts crumpling savagely as they collapsed.

I realised that I had been holding my breath for several moments, until it hurt in my lungs and I released it in a long-drawn-out sigh.

"That's that," I said, speaking almost to myself. "Now let's get out of here before they decide to come after us. We've got to be back in Hayanger before dawn. And there may be patrols on the road now, alerted by the explosions and the gunfire."

"Don't forget," said Svenson tightly, "that they may also have had a radio there at the station, in fact they most certainly would have had one. News of what has happened must have been flashed to their headquarters while we were still inside. They will be sending up reinforcements this very minute, apart from possibly blocking all of the roads leading away from here."

"I know," I nodded. Things could be serious unless our luck continued to hold. "The drivers have their orders to stop for nothing. Any roadblocks and they drive right through them, so I would advise you all to hang on to your seats during the return journey, it's likely to be extremely rough."

It was, however, uneventful. There were no roadblocks. Whether we had merely been fantastically fortunate in that the enemy had not reacted to the situation as swiftly as we had expected; or whether they had considered it unlikely we would take the same route back, it was impossible to tell. But shortly before five in the morning, we left the trucks and made the rest of the way into Hayanger on foot.

My stay in Norway lasted for the best part of eighteen months.

During that time, the resistance movement rose from a set of widely-scattered groups, each under its own leader and fighting its own private battles against the occupying forces, into a coherent army, unified, capable of meeting the Germans on their own ground and soundly defeating them.

There were reprisals as the Germans took hostages in attempts to prevent the Underground movement from spreading, from gaining a hold over the population. But these men, the petriots of Norway, had shown that they could fight, even against overwhelming odds, provided that they had the arms and the ammunition, for they were certainly not lacking in courage. And before I left, on board a British submarine, there seemed to be a change in the ordinary people too.

No longer did they seem to be apathetic, or even pro-Quisling, cowering under the threats of the Nazis. Now they were becoming, more and more, on the side of the Underground. It was as if they had suddenly realised that here, in their midst, was a fighting force to be reckoned with, one which would be ready to fight when the time came to throw the German invaders out of their country. The whole world was now recognised as a testing place and, for them, the time of trial had come. Svenson remained behind in Norway, when I left; his work was there, among his own people, waiting the day of liberation.

CHAPTER FIVE

Second Assignment

COLONEL REDDON rasped the wheel of his lighter noisily, lit his cigarette, then leaned back easily in his chair. He eyed me curiously for a long moment without speaking, then said quietly: "I suppose you're still wondering why I went to all the trouble of pulling you out of Norway, just at the moment when it seemed you were needed there more than ever."

"I'll admit that I was puzzled, sir," I said, looking sombrely at the other. "Things seemed to be going quite nicely when I left, so I presumed that my job there was finished, that Svenson and the others would be able to carry on without my help."

"That's true, in a way. But I'm afraid that there's a little more to it than that. I needed you here for another extremely important assignment. I don't really like having to do this to you after what you've clearly been through during the past year and a half. But it's vitally important and you're the best man we have for the job."

I flicked the grey ash off the end of my cigarette and waited for the other to go on, knowing that there was more to come. But he was silent for a long moment, absorbed in his own thoughts, quiet for so long that I thought he did not intend to continue. Then he straightened up in his chair, stirred himself, and got slowly to his feet, going over to the map which hung on the wall. He jabbed at it with a long forefinger.

"This is where you've been spending the past eighteen months," he said quietly, "but important events have been happening elsewhere, as you probably know. Especially in Europe, down here inside Denmark. Some time ago, possibly you may not have heard of this, an influential Dane named Christmas Moller fled to England and began broadcasting from here to the Danish people. While in Denmark he had been the main instigator behind the founding of an underground paper, *Frit Danmark*. He was actively engaged in resistance activities and there seems to be little doubt that his broadcasts have had the effect of strengthening Danish resistance to the Germans."

"He's still in London, sir?"

"Yes, he's still here. We've been training saboteurs to be parachuted into Denmark. These men have been necessary to provide much-needed leadership." The other drew deeply on his cigarette for a moment, then went on: "You've got to remember that Denmark is a little different from Norway, and especially from countries such as France and Holland. The Communists in Denmark seem to have taken a rather benevolent attitude towards the German occupation of their country, although this attitude changed once Germany attacked Russia. But from the very beginning, back in 1941, the Germans increased their efforts to absorb Denmark into what they termed the New Europe—inaugurating trips to Germany for prominent business men and newspaper editors, trade-union leaders and the like. Arranging too, for scientific institutes to be built. There were several indications at that time that Denmark had decided to accept German occupation, if not willingly, at least without too much trouble on the part of the people."

"But since then there has been this resurgence against Nazism?"

"Exactly. Unfortunately, they may have left things a little too late. They aren't prepared to fight as the French and Norwegians are. The Germans are in an extremely strong position there and it isn't going to be easy building up their resistance movements, or even getting the guns and materials through to them with which they can fight."

"And my job will be to go in there with these other trained saboteurs and teach the Danish patriots how to fight, just as I did in Norway?" I raised my brows slightly, leaning forward with my elbows on the desk.

He shook his head slowly. "Not exactly. We can leave most of that to the others. What I'm asking you to do is to go to Denmark, contact the Underground there and try to contact a man known as Valdemar Larsen."

"Larsen," I repeated the word to myself under my breath.

"That's right. But I think it only fair to warn you here and now that the Germans are also extremely interested in him and would like nothing better than to get their hands on him. If they do, I'm afraid his life won't be worth anything. He's a violent anti-Nazi, one of the leaders of the resistance. But he's also one of their top scientists. We need him in England. The Germans, if they can't get him to work for them, will kill him rather than run the risk of letting him fall into our hands. They know, since Christmas Moller came here, that there are ways and means of getting men out of the country."

"So they'll stop at nothing to prevent him from escaping."

"Exactly. This time, however, you won't be going there by submarine. This time you go into Denmark the hard way. I trust you know how to handle a parachute, Major?"

"I'll admit that I've had very little experience," I said, "but I don't suppose that will alter the fact that I go."

He grinned wryly and stubbed out his cigarette. "I'm afraid not. We want Larsen—we want him badly, just as badly as the Germans do. I have to admit also, that there's little information I can give you which might be of any material help. At the moment, no one seems to know where Larsen is; or even if he's still alive. The last we heard of him was almost seven months ago in a little place near the German frontier called Krusaa, just north of Flensburg. I very much doubt whether he will be there now. When you know that the Germans are hunting you down with every man at their disposal, you don't stay in any one place for any length of time; you keep on the move."

"You're making it sound damnably difficult, sir," I said solemnly.

"I merely thought you ought to have all of the facts at your fingertips," said the other. "At least, you'll know what you're up against."

"I must say I don't look forward to the idea of parachuting into Denmark, but if it's the only way, then that's how it will have to be, I suppose."

"There will be three men going with you, all trained men," said the other briskly. "Once in touch with the resistance, you ought to get some definite information. I won't admit that it will be easy finding Larsen, but if the Resistance movement can't help you, then there's no one on this earth who can."

"And assuming that everything goes according to plan and I do succeed in finding him, sir, how am I to get him back to England?"

"The Resistance will contact us here in London if you succeed, and we will arrange everything from this end. You'll get your instructions then."

I flickered a quick glance at him, then looked away again. "It seems that quite a lot must depend on this one man, sir," I said slowly. "He must be carrying a lot of vital information around in his head."

"He is. Make no mistake about that—and don't underestimate the ability of the Germans to find him. They know that we're landing men in Denmark to help the resistance. And they must surely realise that, sooner or later, we're going to send a man in with the express intention of picking up Larsen."

"But Denmark is a pretty big place, sir," I ventured. "It could take a lifetime to find him. What makes you think I'd have any more success than the Germans who've been looking for him for over seven months and who have several thousand men at their disposal?"

"I'm not at all sure that you will be able to locate him." Reddon shook his head. "But this is about the only chance that we have and we must take it. We can get you both out of Denmark reasonably safely and quickly. But first you have to find him."

I sat silent, said nothing. He's coming to the really sticky bit now, I thought desperately.

"Larsen was a professor at one of the Danish universities before the war. When the Germans occupied the country, they closed down some of the universities, then allowed them to open again, once the Danish Government agreed to co-operate with them. Larsen refused to work under the Nazi regime. He resigned his post at the university and then, as far as we can tell, he virtually vanished off the face of the earth. We've heard of him once or twice since then. How much reliance we can put on the information we received, it's a little hard to tell, even now. Some of it was corroborated by other men inside Denmark."

"But of course it might be possible to——"

"We'll be taking you out in a week from now," went on Reddon. It was very doubtful if he had even heard the interruption. "Everything has been laid on for your benefit. You may not know it, but quite suddenly, you'll find yourself as the centre of attraction. But after your escapades inside Norway, this will come as nothing new to you."

"I wish I could be sure of that, sir," I laughed, but inwardly I was feeling far from amused. "And in the meantime, is there anything for me to do, or do I rate a week's leave?"

Reddon placed the tips of his fingers together. "I think that can be arranged. There isn't much to see in London, I'm afraid. We've had our own troubles here as you probably noticed on your way here. Jerry seems determined to blast us off the map, although during the past few months, he's been switching his attentions around the country."

I nodded, saying nothing. After a brief pause, the other reached beneath the desk and pulled out a slender bottle and a couple of glasses. He broke the seal and poured out two drinks, sliding one of them to me. "Well, that's it, I suppose, Major. Here you are on the brink of another journey overseas. Not in the best traditions of the Army, I think, and you'll get very little recognition for it. But if you do manage to pull it off, I can assure you that His Majesty's Government won't forget you."

"And if I don't?" I looked at him soberly over the rim of the glass.

He shrugged. "They'll treat you as a spy if they catch you. We won't be able to help you. But you know all that. Hell . . . I hate having to ask a man to do something like this. I'd rather be going there myself. In fact, if I were only fifteen years younger, I might try for it."

For long seconds, I looked at the impassive face in front of me, then sipped my drink slowly. It was the real stuff, running smoothly over my tongue and down my throat. I wondered how the other had managed to lay his hands on it; but even in wartime, it seemed there were still ways and means if one only knew them.

Finishing the drink, I rose to my feet. Reddon had not moved. His face was grim, lowered over his drink so that the overhead lights threw it into shadow.

"Will there be anything else, sir?" I asked, after a hesitant pause. For an instant, he did not seem to have heard, then he raised his head sharply.

"No, no, that's all for the moment, my boy," he said harshly. "I'll want to see you here in six days time. Twenty hundred hours on Thursday. Until then, your time's your own."

Reddon had insisted on driving the big Humber himself and sat immobile behind the wheel, his face relaxed on the surface, but giving no outward indication of the turbulent thoughts which were running through his mind. His hands, hard on the wheel, were white-knuckled and he kept his foot hard down on the accelerator. There was little traffic on the road as we left London and headed into the darkness of the open country. The dipped head-lights just managed to pick out details of the road, but for the most part, the rest of the countryside around us flowed past, hidden in a dark billowing cloak of black anonimity.

"You're sure you've got everything now, Major." His voice sounded a trifle tired, but a little of the steel underneath still showed through. He swung the car around a sharp bend, then straightened it out again.

"Yes, sir," I nodded quietly. "The plane will drop us outside Grindsted a little after three o' clock in the morning. We bury our chutes and contact this man Hansen who will be our go-between as far as the local Resistance movement is concerned. Once we're in touch with them, I merely let matters take their course until I can get a lead on the whereabouts of Larsen."

"Good." Reddon stared straight along the dark, winding road, manipulating the powerful car with an almost contemptuous ease. "We've warned Hansen to expect you. He'll be on the look out for you. Nothing should go wrong. This landing site was deliberately chosen for several reasons. All other landings, of agents and trained saboteurs have been made in other parts of the country. We know that the Germans have tightened security there, but they can't possibly watch every square inch of ground and we feel pretty certain that you'll be reasonably safe landing there. But you're the important man here." His voice took on a grimmer edge. "If anything should go wrong when you land, if the Germans do happen to surprise you, the three men with you will hold them off, at the cost of their own lives if necessary so that you'll be able to get away.

"I want you to understand that point quite clearly. If you are attacked, then you will leave, get to hell out of there, leaving the others behind. I don't want any heroics as far as you are concerned. I know this isn't going to be an easy thing to do, and I'm hoping to God that it won't be necessary, but you must leave these men and escape yourself. What you have to do is far more important than the lives of just three men. You understand that, Major?"

For an instant, he turned his face to look at me and I nodded stiffly. "I understand perfectly, sir. The most good, for the most people. That's it, isn't it?" I sighed as the other inclined his head slightly in answer. "This man Larsen must be important if that's the case."

"He is, believe me. If we have to balance the lives of three men against his, then he comes up top every time. I'm afraid I can't tell you why he's so important to us. The less you know about that, the better for all concerned."

Even though the other did not say it outright, I knew the reason behind that statement. If I were captured by the Germans, I would not be able to tell them anything I did not know. I felt a little shiver course through me. So far, I had been fortunate and had not fallen into the hands of the Gestapo, but there had been many stories of what had happened to those who did; and they had not been nice. I stared out through the windscreen, watching the dark, fleeting shapes of the trees as they moved swiftly past on both sides. Reddon seemed to be driving the car purely by guess and by God, for it seemed impossible that he could see the road ahead for more than five or six yards and yet never once did he slacken speed and the needle of the speedometer had remained around the fifty mark ever since we had left the outskirts of London behind.

Before I had gone to Norway, there had always seemed to have been an air of indefinable glamour about landing behind enemy lines, or in enemy-occupied countries, working hand in glove with the Underground. But my illusions had been shattered after that experience in Norway when I had been forced to watch the execution of Collett as a traitor. And it was impossible to tell what

I would find in Denmark. The enemy were clever and utterly ruthless. They had been known to place their own agents inside little groups of the Resistance, so that they knew every move that the patriots made, were ready to swoop and wipe them out without warning.

Less than half an hour later, Reddon slowed the car and I sat upright in my seat, peering through the windscreen. It was getting lighter now, almost dawn and over to our right, I made out the unmistakable shape of Nissen huts and the bulky silhouettes of several aircraft.

"This is the place," said Reddon quietly. "Another twelve hours or so and you should be on your way."

We travelled in silence for the next five minutes as Reddon drove along the outskirts of the airfield, before turning in between two gates flanked by barbed wire. Our identities and passes were checked and then we were inside.

"Your three companions should be waiting for us in the Briefing Room," said Reddon as we drove around the narrow perimeter track to the small group of buildings. "Once you've met them, I expect you'd like something to eat and then some sleep. After being up all night, I reckon you could do with some."

Group-Captain Williams, the C.O. met us at the door of the Briefing Room, shook hands, and then led us inside. The three men, already in the room, rose to their feet and I looked at them closely. Rugged characters, I decided, who would stop at nothing. Colonel Reddon had certainly chosen his men well. I smiled inwardly as the Colonel introduced us. If I were the German Commander, I wouldn't care to be given the job of rounding up such men as these. It was difficult to say why they struck me as being so dangerous. Certainly, there was the look of quiet, confident watchfulness about all three of them. Men of medium height, wiry and tough, with clear blue eyes indicating Scandinavian ancestry, most likely Danish. Professional killers, every one of them, I reflected.

While Reddon briefed us on operations after we had landed in Denmark, I studied the three men with a detached part of my mind. Clausen, who appeared to be the oldest of them, possibly in his late thirties, was short, stockily-built, square-jawed and with piercing blue eyes that seemed to stare through me disquietingly whenever he glanced appraisingly in my direction. Unlike the other two, I had the impression that he was trying to size me up, too, trying inwardly to assess my worth. It gave me a somewhat uncomfortable feeling. The other two, Heinesen and Flaubert sat quiet and relaxed in their chairs, legs crossed, with apparently not a single care in the world. From the expression on their faces, it was impossible to believe that they would soon be going out on one of the most dangerous missions of their lives.

"I'm not going to attempt to underestimate, or play down, the difficulties that you're going to encounter once you land," finished Reddon softly. His voice seemed as calm and as matter-of-fact as ever. "This isn't a suicide mission I'm sending you out upon—but the Germans are wary now. We know they've captured one or two of our agents and as far as they're concerned, being forewarned is being forearmed. Apart from that, unless the Underground know where to find Larsen, it's going to be like looking for a needle in the proverbial haystack. Larsen is hiding from the Germans. He knows that his life is at stake and a man with that knowledge is not going to be the easiest person to find; and even if you do find him, it won't be easy to persuade him to go with you. He can trust no one. Even among members of the Resistance, there may be men in the pay of the enemy who will turn him over to the Gestapo even when they claim that they're doing their best to smuggle him out of the country. But I'll leave that particular bridge to you when you come to it. For the time being, you'll have all of your work cut out trying to locate him."

When he had finished, there were no questions. Reddon turned to the Group-Captain, standing near the door. The other gave a brief nod. "The plane is all ready for tonight, Colonel. I've got my best crew standing by, ready to take these gentlemen to their point of rendezvous." He smiled thinly. "I can't even guarantee them a comfortable crossing. Jerry has been building up his anti-aircraft batteries in that area and we know that he's transferred one or two fighter squarions to Denmark during the past six months. But we'll do our best to get them there safely."

I slept little during that afternoon, even though my body was tired from lack of sleep. When I finally woke after an uneasy doze, it was with a sense of dull apprehension, the feeling that somewhere in the near future, danger was building up for me. Outside, it was getting dusk. Clouds were lying low on the eastern horizon, stretching across it in long dark bars and the sun, setting in the west had a pale, yellow glow about it which presaged bad weather.

The feeling of impending disaster remained with me, in the background of my mind, as I ate a hasty meal in the Mess and then followed the three Danes out to the waiting aircraft. The crew were already on board and gave us the thumbs-up sign as we climbed inside the aircraft and settled down into our places.

The co-pilot, a stocky, red-haired Scotsman, gave us a friendly grin. "I won't ask you what your mission is going to be," he said, a soft burr to his words, "but our orders are to take you out over Denmark and drop you south-west of Grindsted. I suggest you make yourselves comfortable. According to the Met boys, the weather is going to break down at any moment and they're anticipating strong head winds over the dropping zone."

I nodded briefly. "That's probably going to be the easiest part of this operation just so long as you get us there in one piece."

"We'll do that, have no fear. Remember, we're in this plane too." He leaned casually against the radio transmitter. "You know, this situation reminds me of a story

I heard once. About some poor devil going to the gallows, walking across the prison yard in the pouring rain with the chaplain, grumbling about the weather. And the Chaplain told him that——"

"I know," I said, a little more sharply than I had intended. "The prisoner was lucky. He didn't have to walk back through it. I guess that's what we feel like now. No need to remind us."

"Sorry." The other still had a cheerful grin on his face. He waited in silence for a few more moments, then said quickly. "Well, I suppose I'd better get back up front. We'll be taking off in a little while. Make yourselves at home."

"Thanks," I said dryly. "We'll do our best."

"Take no notice of him," drawled the radio operator, when the co-pilot had gone. "He always tries to see the funny side of things. One of these nights, we're going to run into real trouble out there, and then he isn't going to think it so funny." He settled down in front of the transmitter, easing himself more comfortably into his seat. A few moments later, the engines burst into uproarious life, the plane shuddered convulsively like a living thing.

The plane moved forward slowly around the perimeter track, the muted roar of the powerful engines never changing. Then we stopped.

"What's happened now?" I asked thinly.

"No need to worry, sir." The radio operator turned his head, grinning. "We're at the end of the runway, waiting for the take-off signal from Control."

"Oh," I forced myself to relax. This, I told myself, was even worse than being on board that submarine, heading for Norway. The note of the engines changed abruptly. The plane began to roll forward, slowly at first, but gaining momentum. How long the shuddering, straining sensation continued it was impossible for me to estimate, but quite suddenly, almost before I was aware of it, the shaking ceased, there was the curious sensation of being suspended in mid-air.

"Airborne," said the operator without turning his head. "We're turning on to course." There was no emotion in his voice.

Ten minutes later, the co-pilot came through. "Would you care to go up front?" he asked. "Everything is purely routine until we reach our objective. Or unless we run into a bunch of Messerschmitts."

"Do you reckon that's likely?" I asked as I got to my feet, stretched my legs and followed him towards the pilot's cabin.

The other pursed his lips. "We can't be sure. There's a big raid scheduled for tonight on Bremen. It may help to draw off most of their fighters, giving us a clear run through. On the other hand, if they spot us on their radar, a single plane flying over Denmark, they'll put two and two together and blast us with everything they've got. When it comes to a thing like that, you toss the coin and take your choice. If we don't run into them on the way in, I reckon there's a distinct possibility that they'll hit us on the way back."

I entered the pilot's cabin and looked around me at the myriad switches and dials which lay spread out in front of the pilot. He gave me a friendly grin and indicated the seat beside him. "Take a pew, Major," he said genially. "I suppose all this must be pretty dull for you fellows. But if we do run into trouble and for your sakes, I hope that we don't, things will liven up no end."

"Where are we now?" I asked, peering through the cockpit, trying to make out details from the blurred darkness below.

"Just approaching the coast. We'll be over it in about ten minutes."

Down below, I could see nothing. Details seemed to appear and then fade again, tantalisingly, but finally, at the corner of my vision, I made out a thin line of white, a demarkation line which I knew instinctively was the dividing line between land and water. Then we were out over the sea and England lay behind us. For a moment, I felt a sickening sense of loss, and wondered if, and when, I would ever see it again. The future was suddenly a very uncertain thing.

The journey over the sea was uneventful. It was impossible to see any details in the flat, featureless blankness which lay below us. Flying at an altitude of two thousand feet, we crossed the Danish coast and flew inland. This, I told myself, was where trouble would come. As far as I knew, there had been very few, if any, raids on Denmark by the R.A.F. since it had been taken over by the Nazis; and it seemed unlikely that the Germans would divert any of their previous anti-aircraft batteries and fighter squadrons there, in spite of what Colonel Reddon had told us. There would, however, be radar stations there, watching the air, plotting our course.

The minutes passed slowly, until it was ready for us to go, time to strap on our chutes, check our weapons, and prepare for the drop.

"All set?" The co-pilot gave us a brief glance. "We're almost there. Another three minutes, if we can trust the calculations of our navigator."

I nodded, stared down into the stygian well of blackness which yawned at my feet, my hands clinging tightly to the side of the plane as the blast of air, screaming in through the opening in the side of the aircraft tugged at my body and threatened to suck me out. I could make out nothing down there. It was impossible to tell how high we were. Two thousand feet according to the pilot, but as far as vision was concerned, it could have been two thousand miles.

I was aware of the other three men, crouched behind me, their faces in shadow. What were the thoughts running through their minds at that moment? I wondered. Once I hit the ground, my orders were to get away as quickly as possible, locate this man known as Hansen. Through him I would contact the Underground which was quite well organised in this area. But if there was trouble, it was quite likely that none of these three men would live until the dawn. Their role was that of a body-guard for me. But if they felt anything of this very real and fundamental difference between us, they gave no cutward sign.

"Now!" yelled the co-pilot sharply. The single word jarred through my brain, holding me rigid for a brief fraction of a second before my muscles galvanised themselves into action. Without pausing to think, I hurled myself forward into the blackness, aware of the terrible sick feeling in the pit of my stomach. There was an almost irresistible urge to pull the ripcord, but with a supreme effort, I resisted it. When I finally did pull it, there was a bried moment of panic, when it seemed that the chute had failed. I had a momentary vision of crashing into the ground somewhere below, of being killed before I had a chance of getting to grips with the enemy. Then there was a savage tug across my shoulders and I was no longer falling free but dangling at the end of the chute. Oh God, I thought quietly, I even remembered to count.

Of the moments that followed, there remained only a chaotic jumble of half-remembered events. Of the ground appearing suddenly out of the formless, featureless darkness beneath me, of the instinctive bracing of the muscles of my legs, of remembering to bend my knees and roll forward the moment I hit the ground with a jarring crash that almost knocked me cold. Then the spilling of air from the chute before it could drag me over the uneven ground and the mad scramble to gather it up into a small bundle before pausing even to look around for the others.

Finally, sucking air down into my tortured lungs, I got slowly to my feet and scuttled for the low hedge in the distance. We had landed in a wide field. There was a clump of trees at one corner and one of the chutes was already drifting down towards them. There was no sign of the other two and I guessed that they had already landed.

Reaching the hedge, I thrust the folded chute into the bottom, below the surface of dark, muddy water, treading it in with the heel of my boot. It would be discovered sometime by the enemy, but before then, I hoped to be several miles away. Not until this task was finished, did I move swiftly towards the clump of trees. As I approached them, a dark figure rose up out of the underbrush and confronted me. It was Clausen.

"Are you all right, Major?" he asked in a low voice.

"Yes, I'm fine. What about the others? Any sign of them?"

"I think they came down in the other field, a couple of hundred yards away in that direction," he pointed. "I watched you land and decided to wait for you before going to look for them. Now that you're all right, we'll see if we can find them. The sooner we get away from here, the safer it will be for all of us."

With moon and stars blanketed by the heavy, low cloud, visibility was almost nil. Indeed, it was scarcely more than twenty feet in any direction. Very slowly and cautiously, we made our way forward, making as little noise as possible.

We had reached the edge of the other field were on the point of pushing our way through it, oblivious to the thorns which clutched at our flesh and clothing, when a sudden sharp burst of gunfire broke out in the near distance. Instantly, I threw myself down into the icy-cold water in the ditch, holding my breath, pulling the pistol from my belt.

"A German patrol," I hissed. "Where in hell's name did that come from? And how did they know we were here?"

"It's quite simple," muttered Clausen bitterly. "They must have been tracking the plane by radar, following it all the way here. They would know that a solitary plane would not be heading as far as this unless it was on an important mission."

I felt a wave of futile anger pass swiftly through me. This was the one possibility that Colonel Reddon had foreseen, had warned me about. His orders had been explicit then, but now that the moment had actually arrived, now that the German fire was being answered from two points in the field where Heinesen and Flaubert were crouched under cover, I knew that it would be difficult to obey those orders and leave these men to certain death—or worse, if they were captured alive.

I brought up the pistol, my finger tightening on the trigger, but Clausen caught my arm and pulled it down again, urgently. "No," he hissed thinly. "The others will hold them off until we make a get away. It's only a small patrol. It's possible that the Germans had them strung out along the extrapolated route they calculated for the plane, so that they would be ready for any emergency. We must get away as quickly as possible. No noise, or we're finished."

"But Heinesen and Flaubert," I protested harshly. "We can't leave them there like this. If it's only a small group of Germans, we may be able to kill them all if we take them from the flank."

"There's no time for that. The shooting will have attracted attention."

"Don't try to stop me," I said dangerously, making up my mind. "Orders or no orders, I'm going to help the others." I pushed myself forward a couple of inches, slipping the safety catch off the pistol.

The other was very calm and quiet. "That will solve nothing," he said insistently. "You are the one man who has to remain alive. Both of the others know this. They knew it when they set out. Do you want them both to die for nothing? We have to find Larsen and get him out of the country, back to England. That is the only important thing, that is above our lives."

"All right, all right," I nodded my head savagely and jerked my arm away from his restraining hand. "I'll come with you." I was back on balance once again, realising with a sudden clarity that what the other said was true. There was no other alternative for me. I had to go and leave those two men to die. It was possible that unless the enemy searched the area very thoroughly, or had seen us come down, they might take it for granted that only two men had landed from that plane and they would look no further. Even if they did, the chances were that we would have contacted the Resistance through Hansen before they caught up with us.

Noicelessly, we slipped away through the long, wet grass, reached a narrow cart-track on the opposite side of the low hedge beneath which I had hidden my parachute, and struck off in a south-westerly direction, checking with the small compass every five minutes. Behind us, the firing flared up swiftly to a sudden crescendo, then stopped altogether. I felt a sickening sensation in the pit of my stomach, a feeling of loss. I had known those two men for less than two days, knew scarcely anything about their backgrounds, their past lives. And yet they had somehow become a part of me. For a brief moment in this terrible war, they had been closer to me than friends, than relatives. They had shared a part of my life which could never be forgotten, which was etched indelibly in my mind.

We moved as quickly as we dared during the next two hours. It was almost five o'clock. Soon it would be light and further travel would be not only dangerous, but virtually impossible. For all we knew, the Germans had patrols out at that very moment, scouring the countryside, searching for us. I doubted if either of the two men we had left behind would have talked, even if they had been taken alive.

"How long before we reach this farm?" I asked finally, turning to Clausen. In the darkness, it was difficult to correlate landmarks with those on the map which I had memorised before leaving England. I had the feeling that without Clausen, I might have been hopelessly lost by now, but he seemed to know his way around with an unerring instinct.

"Not far. We should reach it before dawn. There's just the possibility that the Germans know of it too and may be watching the place. We must be careful."

"How could they know about it?" I asked. "You think

that attack back there was something more than a coincidence or a lucky chance on their part?"

"Not necessarily. They could just possibly have picked up the message for Hansen telling him to expect us. They've broken our codes before, you know."

"You think they suspect?"

He shrugged. "It's possible. I believe in taking no chances, Major. The Germans are a clever and completely ruthless race. If they do know we're here, you can be quite sure that as far as we are concerned, they won't show their hand until we've led them to the other members of the Resistance in this area. They don't just want to capture us, they're after bigger stakes."

It was still dark, with the dawn just beginning to light up the eastern horizon by the time we came out of a small wood and looked down upon the peaceful scene in front of us. The farmhouse where Hansen lived stood a little way back from the secondary road, between two clumps of tall trees. There was no sign of life even at that distance and I examined every inch of the surrounding terrain for any evidence that the Germans were there, watching the place, waiting for us to arrive. Finally, I was satisfied. "There's no one watching the farm," I said confidently.

"It ought to be safe enough to go in. We can't stay out here all day."

Clausen hesitated for a moment, then nodded in agreement."Are you sure that it's perfectly safe?"

"Damnit to hell, I'm certainly positive about nothing. But there are some calculated risks that we have to take, and this is one of them."

Keeping under cover most of the way, we entered one of the clumped groups of trees, examined the farmhouse from close quarters, then moved forward. We had almost reached it when a dog barked sharply. I brought up the short barrel of the pistol instantly then relaxed my finger on the trigger as a dark figure moved into view from around the corner of the house. There was a rifle in his hand, a rifle which was pointed directly at my stomach.

"Hansen!" Clausen spoke the word quickly.

"Who are you?" The rifle never wavered by so much as an inch and I knew that if we did not satisfy this man as to our identity, he would not hesitate to shoot.

"Clausen," said my companion in a harsh voice. "We come from Colonel Reddon in London. You got his message?"

The other nodded in satisfaction, lowered the rifle, still holding it tight in his right hand and came forward. He stretched out his left hand and said something sharply to the dog. "You are on time," he murmured quietly. "What happened to the others. Colonel Reddon mentioned four men."

"We were attacked just after landing,"I said heavily. "They stayed behind to hold them off while we came out here."

"You were not followed?" It was more of a statement than a question.

I shook my head. "I'm positive that we weren't. But we weren't sure whether Germans were watching the farm. That's why we came so silently."

The other smiled as he motioned us forward. "I spotted you ten minutes ago." he said proudly. "It is fortunate that the Germans are not as sharp-sighted as I."

There was no malice in the other's voice as he took us inside. He gestured towards the chairs in front of the fire in the wide hearth. "You'll be hungry and tired, I expect." he said. "I'll get you something to eat and then we can talk."

Five minutes later, we sat down to breakfast. I ate quickly, realising for the first time just how hungry I really was. There was a deep-seated weariness in my body and every nerve and muscle ached continuously. I tried to question Hansen while we ate, but he merely waved an arm and indicated that there would be time enough to talk once we had eaten.

Finally, I could eat no more and sat back in my seat.

"Now," I said quietly, "tell us what you know of Larsen. If we are to find him, we'll need every scrap of information that we can get. We know that the Germans are trying to find him, that they've been hunting for him for many months. But what have the Resistance been doing all of that time?"

"We haven't been idle. We knew of the manhunt that was on for Larsen, although none of us knew why the Germans wanted him so badly. For all we knew, he was just another intellectual who resented the presence of the Nazis here and who seemed determined to have nothing to do with them. But as far as we knew, he had not actually fought against them, he was not in the Resistance movement, had never even fired a shot against them. So it seemed that there had to be something else which was prompting this strange interest in him."

"And?"

"We finally assumed that he had valuable information which the Germans wanted and that it was imperative that they should find him before he gave that information to the Allies. When we received the message from London warning us that you were on your way to Denmark to pick him up and smuggle him out of the country, back to England, our assumption seemed to be correct."

CHAPTER SIX

The Search and the Goal

"LARSEN *is* important to us," I confirmed. "There seems to be a widely-held opinion that if the Germans do capture him, they'll kill him rather than take the risk of him falling into our hands."

"Do you know what kind of information he has?" asked the other pointedly. He eyed me shrewdly, brows drawn bar-straight across his forehead.

"No. I'm afraid that I don't. They considered that it was possibly better for me not to know, just in case my luck ran out and I was captured too. The Gestapo have special methods of extracting information from unwilling prisoners, I understand." I gave a quick nod. "But at the moment, the important thing is: How do we set about finding him before the Germans do?"

"That will not be too difficult," said the other and there was a touch of unmistakable pride in his tone. "We have not been idle, as I said earlier. We now know where he is hiding. But——" He held up one hand as I started to my feet. "I do not want you to think that your troubles are over. Far from it. Although we know where he is, we have not yet contacted him. We thought it best to wait until you arrived. He may not listen, even to you. For all he knows, it could be a trap, a trick to get him to Germany where he would live for only a few days and at the end of that time, if the Gestapo had their way, he would be pleading for death.

"I think you understand what I am saying. Why Larsen will not be an easy man to persuade. Besides, we must take care that we do not lead the Germans there. They have spies everywhere. It is difficult to know who to trust these days."

"I understand," I said grimly. "But if we can only get to him, I think I might be able to prove to him who I am."

"I only hope that you are right, Major. I will give you all the help I can."

"Thank you. There's the possibility that the Germans may intensify their search now that they know there was a parachute landing during the night and——" I froze into an attitude of listening immobility, turning my head slightly at the sudden sound from outside. Gently, every movement quiet and smooth, I pulled the loaded pistol from my belt, lining the barrel up on the door, but Hansen merely smiled and rose to his feet. "It will be one of the others," he said casually.

"How do you know?" I spoke harshly, unable to relax even in the face of his calm assurance. "It could be anyone snooping around."

"Perhaps. But there are only a few people can come here without my dog barking. He is better than a look-out. He never makes a mistake."

A moment later, there was the sound of heavy footsteps just outside the door, and someone knocked loudly. Going forward, Hansen opened the door, stood to one side as three men entered. Tall, lean men, grim and efficient-looking, they came into the room and eyed us carefully from beneath lowered brows.

"These are two of the men we were told to expect, Hansen?" asked of them in a low voice.

The farmer nodded his head quickly. "These are they." He spoke rapidly. "There were four of them but the other two were killed when a German patrol attacked."

"We know that." The man seated himself at the table, not once taking his eyes off us. "You seek Larsen?" he asked.

"That's right." I gave a quick, brief nod. "I understand that you know where he is. Can you take us to him?"

"Perhaps. First I want to know why it is that you wish to smuggle him out of Denmark. He is merely a school-teacher."

"A professor at one of the universities," I corrected.

"So? A professor. But that alters nothing. Why should London be so interested in him?" There was no emotion in the flat, toneless voice, but I felt an odd sense of un-easiness. There was something about the other which I could not quite place. A fanatical look in his dark eyes, it was true, but it went deeper than that.

"I'm afraid I can't answer that," I said slowly, feeling a trifle angry at this unexpected questioning. "But why are you asking all of this. We can prove who we are *if* it's that which is troubling you. Do you think that we're German agents, put here to spy on you?"

"That has happened before," went on the other harshly. "But no, I'm quite satisfied that you are a British agent. I simply wish to know why Larsen is so important to you. Or are you trying to keep something from us?"

"For God's sake," I burst out suddenly, angrily. "We haven't time to go into the whys and wherefores of all this. My orders are to contact you, reach this man and smuggle him out of the country. If you have any other ideas, then I suggest that you get in touch with London yourselves. I'm quite sure they can straighten you out on one or two points."

"The metaphor eludes me at the moment," continued the other, unruffled, quite unperturbed. "You do not wish to tell me then?"

"I can't tell you because I simply don't know," I said wearily, wondering where this line of conversation was going to end. "Now, are you going to help us or not?"

The other pursed his lips into a tight line, then turned to his two companions. I could read nothing in the glance he threw them, but after a brief pause he nodded his head. "Very well, I'm satisfied that you are telling the truth. We will take you to where he is said to be hiding. If you can persuade him to go with you, then we will contact London and make the necessary arrangements."

"When do we go?" I asked impatiently. I was now anxious to get this thing over with as soon as possible. The news that these people knew where Larsen was hiding was more than I had ever dared hope for. But it was a little difficult to understand the other's attitude.

"We will make the arrangements and then contact you again," said the other, getting to his feet. "In the meantime, may I suggest that you remain here. You will be quite safe. Hansen is a man we can trust and I do not think that the German patrols will worry you unduly out here. Even if they do, Hansen has many places where he can hide you." He gave the farmer an enigmatic glance, then walked towards the door.

When he had gone, when the sound of their footsteps had died away, I turned to the other. "There's something about him that I don't like," I said thinly. "Are you sure that *he* can be trusted?"

Hansen nodded unhappily. "He hates the Germans, probably more than the rest of us, but he is a strange one is Nielson and his politics make him as ruthless as the enemy, if not more so."

"His politics?" I queried. "I'm afraid that I don't understand."

"I'm sorry, I thought you had realised. Nielson is an ardent Communist. He takes his orders, if he ever receives any, from Moscow. That is why he is so anxious to know about Larsen. If this man is important, he wonders if Russia ought not to know about it first."

"I must confess that the thought had never occurred to me," I admitted. "But now that you mention it, it explains a lot of things. And those two men with him?"

"The same. You'll find that a great part of the men in the Underground in Denmark are Communists. They threw in their lot with the Germans when they first took over control of our country, but turned against them when Hitler attacked Russia. As for myself, I do not trust them too much. They have allegiance not to Denmark, but to

Russia. When this war is over and our country is free again, we must be careful, otherwise we may find that we have spawned a devil in our midst."

"First we must win the war," I said soberly. "How long do you think they will keep us waiting?"

The other gave a negligent shrug of his shoulders. "That is impossible to tell. When they say that they will arrange things, it means that they will try to find out everything they can about you and your mission here before they commit themselves."

"I see. That's just fine," I sank back into my chair, filled with a sense of anger and frustration. Colonel Reddon had not mentioned anything like this during our briefing. I had the inescapable feeling that the Communists were merely stringing us along, and the thought merely intensified my anger. Did these people not realise that Clausen and I were risking our lives to help them? That two good men had already died so that we might succeed.

But the anger did not last. There was nothing that we could do to hurry things along and I resigned myself to the fact that all we could do was wait and keep ourselves out of sight.

Hansen lived alone at the farm with only his dog for company and we soon learned that on the side, he traded with the Germans and by this means, was able to prevent any suspicion falling upon him and also could obtain bits of information which it might have been impossible to get from other sources. Being on friendly terns with the German Kommandant in the area, also meant that he could travel the countryside in his battered old truck without hindrance, any troops who stopped him accepting his explanation that he was merely delivering more supplies for the Kommandant.

On the second day of our stay at the farm, we learned the fate of our two companions. Hansen's face was grave as he told us the news. "One of them was killed during the fighting," he explained; "but the other was taken alive, although severely wounded. As far as I've been able to gather, he was taken into Grindsted for treatment. Then he will he questioned as soon as he is in a fit condition to answer questions. The Gestapo are here, that much is certain."

"Just as I thought," I said thickly. "I doubt whether he will talk. Even if he does, he can only tell them about Clausen and myself."

"Does he know about Larsen?" asked Hanson, peering closely into my face.

"Yes, I'm afraid that he does, although he doesn't know why we want him so desperately. But even that titbit of information will give the Germans an idea of why we're here. We must work fast if we're to stand any chance of success. Do you think you can get word through to Neilson and his friends. Tell him that the Gestapo have one of the men who landed with us and that it won't be long before they get valuable information out of him. We must move soon, tonight if it's at all possible."

"I'll see him right away," promised the other. "I think I know where to find him. But whether or not he will agree, I do not know."

"He has to agree," I said sharply. "We have our orders too. Tell him that if he doesn't, we'll start looking for Larsen ourselves, and that we'll get in touch with other groups of the Resistance for help in locating him. That might move him."

"Perhaps." The other did not seem too happy about the idea. "But Neilson is a hard man and a bad man to threaten."

"Just tell him what I've told you," I said thinly. "I'll take the consequences if he tries to get rough. Tell him that he'll have to answer to those in London if he refuses to help us."

Hansen was gone for the best part of three hours. During that time, I waited impatiently. In spite of my air of confidence earlier that morning, I did not feel so sure of myself. If he thought that we were holding out on him, it was quite on the cards that Neilson would not help us, or would try to put obstacles in our way. There was little trust between the Communists and the democratic Danes, even though both were dedicated to fighting the same enemy. Whereas all that the ordinary Dane wanted was a return to freedom, an end to the war; the Communist look further into the future, to a time when Communism would be the dominant factor in world affairs. Everything had, even now, to be subordinated to that one aim, to making certain that the democratic people of the west should not have any adventage over Russia when the war came to an end.

I looked at my watch. It was almost midday. Hansen should be back soon, I decided. Outside, the countryside basked in warm sunlight and there was no sign of life as far as the eye could see. It was an almost idyllic scene and looking at it, the war and everything connected with it seemed terribly far away. Then, in the distance, I heard a sudden drone and a moment later, a flight of aircraft passed almost directly overhead. Perhaps it wasn't so far away, after all, I reflected. Although here, in Denmark, the presence of German troops was not as noticeable as it had been in Norway, the country was still under the iron heel of the enemy and there was danger everywhere. It meant that if we had to travel at all, it would have to be at night. Hansen would probably use the truck. Several times in the past, so he had told us proudly, he had travelled at night, in spite of the curfew which the enemy often imposed. If he had done it once, then he could do it again without running the risk of having his truck searched.

At half-past twelve, Hansen returned and closed the door softly behind him.

"Well?" I asked, as he seated himself at the rough, wooden table. "What did he say?"

"He hadn't heard about one of the men having been taken alive?" explained the other, pouring himself a cupful of wine. "He said that his information had been that both men had been killed during the fighting. He was very angry when I assured him that the news was true. He does not like to be wrong about anything as you can imagine. But he has agreed that, in the circumstances, we should act at once. He will be here a little after dark tonight, with two of his men. We will take the truck into Aastrup. That is only a few miles to the south of here."

He drained his cup, set it down on the table. "Neilson is certain that he can find him, but there have been several German patrols in the town during the past week. It is possible that they, too, know that Larsen is there. We may run into trouble. I'm telling you this so that you will be ready in case we are stopped."

I nodded in slow understanding. "We'll be ready," I said.

By nightfall, everything was in readiness. Neilson arrived, as unsmiling and taciturn as I had remembered him earlier, the same two men with him as had accompanied him on his last visit. While Hansen busied himself with the old truck, piling boxes of supplies into the back as camouflage in the event of anyone stopping us, I drew Neilson on one side and said urgently. "I think it only fair to warn you that I intend to take Larsen back with me no matter what happens. I know that you're disturbed by the fact that he may have knowledge which would be of vital importance to your Party, but we're fighting a war against the Germans now and it's the Nazi ideology which we have to smash, otherwise there'll be no place for Communism or Democracy in the world."

He looked at me in silence for a few moments, only the smouldering dark eyes giving any indication as to the nature of the thoughts running through his mind. Then he shrugged. "It is as you say, Major. Whatever happens, we must destroy Hitler and all that he stands for. When all this is finished, then there will be a time for reckoning. We shall see then what happens."

"All right," I sighed. "We'll wait until then. But whatever happens, I wanted to make sure that you were with us whole-heartedly in this. We cannot afford to fight among ourselves. That way, none of us will survive."

He grunted something inaudible under his breath and turned sharply away. I watched his retreating back as he strode off towards Hansen. "He is a dangerous one, that," said Clausen softly. "He will bear watching."

"Do you think that he hates us so much that he would turn us over to the Germans?" I asked tensely. It was a thought that had been troubling me for the past two days, but one which I had not wanted to put into words.

"Perhaps. Who know. If the stakes were high enough, I think he would even do that. But somehow, I do not think so."

"I'm glad to hear it. I wouldn't like to have a gun in my back and the Germans in front of me. The odds seem to be lengthening against us every minute. I wonder if Colonel Reddon knew of this when he sent us out here."

"I doubt it. If he had, he would surely have warned us, made sure that we were on our guard against these men."

I nodded briefly, then went forward at a sharp call from Hansen. One after the other, we climbed into the back of the truck, crouching down among the boxes and barrels which Hansen had stacked into the back. It would have required a sharp eye to see that, in spite of the look of randomness about them, there was a definite purpose in the way they had been placed so carefully, that five men could hide among them in the smallest possible space.

It was cramped among the supplies and as the truck jolted forward, I told myself that we were in for a very uncomfortable journey.

It was. The truck seemed to jolt and bounce every few yards as the ancient motor whined and wheezed, threatening to break down at any moment. The heavy boxes too, had not been roped into place and kept shifting and sliding against our bodies, at times threatening to crush us. At the end of half an hour, I felt as though I had been battered mercilessly from head to foot. My body was bruised and sore and the sharp pincers of cramp had clawed their way into my legs so that every moment was a lifetime of agony as my muscles knotted into hard, agonising masses of flesh. It was impossible to stretch my legs to relieve the pain and I was forced to lie there, clenching my teeth to prevent myself from crying out aloud with the agony. Only the fact that Neilson and his men were crouched there, somewhere in the darkness, prevented me from doing so, but to have shown any pain in front of them was the last thing I wanted to do.

Once, on the road, we were stopped and there was the sound of guttural voices close at hand questioning Hansen. It was impossible to hear what they were saying but there was the sound of someone coming around to the back of the truck and a second later, the heam of a flashlight probed the boxes and there was the brief metallic clatter of a bayonet being thrust into one of the sacks, conveniently placed near the tailboard of the truck. Apparantly satisfied, we were allowed to proceed and I exhaled slowly in sudden relief. If that German soldier had been a little more determined or unbelieving. . . .

When the truck stopped again, there were no voices, merely a deep and clinging silence. I crouched there for several moments until Hansen's voice reached me from the back of the truck. "All right. You can come out now. But for God's sake, no noise!"

I rose stiffly to my feet, rubbing the muscles of my legs in an attempt to bring back the circulation. When it did return, the pain was even worse than the numbing cramp which had assailed me for most of the journey. Pins and needles shot through my flesh, almost crippling me. With an effort, I lowered myself out of the truck and stood for a moment, looking about me. There were houses all around us, houses in which not a single light showed. Evidently, we were in the outskirts of Aastrup. So far, so good, I thought. Now what happened?

Neilson took over command. In spite of my suspicions of him, there was little doubt that he knew exactly what he was doing. As yet, there were no indications that anyone had heard the approach of the truck. The normal inhabitants of the town were probably all in their beds by now, either asleep, or not caring what went on outside possibly thinking that it was merely a German army vehicle. As for any German patrols, there did not seem to be any of them around and not wishing to question our obvious good luck, I followed Neilson quickly and noiselessly as he darted across the narrow street and went to ground in the shadows on the opposite side.

I shivered in an icy gust of wind, pushed myself closer in to the wall. My watch told me that it was nearly midnight. Beside me, Cláusen and Hansen lay in one of the doorways, dark shadows, scarcely visible, only the white blur of their features showing up in the darkness.

Neilson motioned us forward again and we moved quickly along the darkened street ears and eyes alert for the faintest sound or movement. My mind felt oddly clear, almost unnaturally so, as if some drug had been administered to me which had lifted the veil of weariness which had earlier pervaded the whole of my body and mind. The feeling of cramp had gone and I felt tensed and eager as if all of my faculties had been sharpened. Swiftly, my mind worked ahead, assessing the position as I knew it, weighing every possibility according to the chances it gave us of success. The heavy pistol in my pocket and the knowledge that we were no longer merely sitting around doing nothing, merely waiting for something to happen, that we were doing something concrete, made me forget the aches and bruises in my body, although I was still remotely aware of them, but with a diminished awareness, as if they belonged to some other person.

I knew that the change from weariness to sharpened mental and physical ability was a psychological change rather than a physiological one and that it was something, like a stiff shot of benzedrine, for which I would have to pay later. But for the time being, I knew that I could cope with the situation.

Neilson reached the end of the street, paused for a moment to check the darkness around him, then waved us forward again. A quarter of an hour after leaving the truck, we lay crouched at the end of a narrow street which lay like a river of midnight in front of us. Not a single light showed there, nothing moved among the shadows.

"Is this the place?" I asked, turning to Neilson. Common sense told me that if Larsen were hiding out anywhere in Aastrup, then it would be in a place like this, away from the middle of the town, a place of shadows and anonymity, a place where a man stood a good chance of losing him self in the eyes of the world, a place where a terribly frightened man might seek refuge.

"This is where we heard he was hiding," corrected Neilson. "He may not still be here, of course. The Germans are searching the area and they may have frightened him off. If so, then we may never find him."

Was there a note of hopeful anticipation in the other's tone? I tried to tell myself that there wasn't, that I had merely imagined it; but I couldn't be sure.

"Which house?" I asked quietly, staring into the dimness.

Neilson pointed to the house a third of a way along the street. There was a small plot of waste ground behind it which I noticed instantly. I nodded. "We ought to be able to reach it without being seen," I said carefully. "I think that someone ought to stay here on watch, just in case a German patrol does happen along while we're in there. Besides, I'm not sure what kind of a welcome we'll get from him, if we do find him there. He may shoot first and ask questions later, you can't account for the actions of a frightened man."

"That's true," agreed Neilson. "I will go with you. The others will stay here until we come back. If there is any trouble, then they know what to do."

"I'm sure they do." I accepted his offer to accompany me without any sign of emotion, although the reason behind it was perfectly clear to me. He wanted to be around when I met Larsen, to satisfy himself as to what went on between us; and also by leaving his men with

Hansen, he could watch him at the same time.

Together, we darted across the dark road, flung ourselves down in the bushes which dotted the waste ground at the back of the house. Cautiously, we got to our feet again and picked our way forward, a few yards at a time, keeping a wary eye on the houses in front of us, our weapons ready in our hands.

We reached the back of the house without incident. The silence around us was oppressive and had a waiting quality which rubbed at my nerves. I wondered whether I ought to have left Hansen with those two killers of Neilson's, then shrugged the thought away. I had had no choice in the matter and it was doubtful if they would kill him. There might be rivalry between the two groups of the Resistance, but they were all Danes, they all wished to see the end of Nazi occupation. The time for trouble would come with the end of the war. I was suddenly thankful that I had only to get Larsen and take him back to England with me. The problems of Denmark after the war would have nothing to do with me.

"Inside—quickly!" Neilson's voice jerked me out of my reverie. He had the back door open, although how he had managed it I did not know. Noiselessly, I stepped inside and he followed close on my heel, closing the door gently behind him. "Now—upstairs! That's where he'll be if he is here."

Catlike, he padded up the narrow stairs, without waiting to see if I were following him. Reaching the top, he paused, motioned me towards one of the two room and made for the other door.

Now that we were there, there was no time for finesse. For all we knew, Larsen might be armed and ready to shoot anyone who came bursting into his room at night. I could imagine how he must be feeling and I knew that in his position, I would not have hesitated to shoot any intruder. Putting my foot to the door, I twisted the handle with one hand, then kicked it open, stepping swiftly to one side as I went in. The room was in darkness, but there was sufficient light to show the man lying on the bed at the far side of the room. He came awake instantly, animal-like in his lightning reactions. His right hand dived beneath the pillow, but my voice pulled him up sharply. "Keep quite still, Larsen," I said thinly. "We haven't come to kill you."

Blinking, he withdrew his hand slowly from beneath the pillow as I went forward. "Who are you? What do you want with me?" he asked and there was a little tremor in his voice.

Reaching down, I slipped the gun from beneath the pillow and put it into my pocket. "There's better," I said softly. "Now we can talk."

Neilson came into the room, stood looking down at the man on the bed. "So you found him," he said tonelessly. "He doesn't look so important to me. Only a frightened rabbit of a man, sleeping with a gun under his pillow. Are you sure this is the man you're looking for?"

"I think so," I turned to the other and said sharply: "I'm from London. I was parachuted into Denmark to find you and take you back with me. There's no need to be afraid. Colonel Reddon will answer any questions you have once we get you back to England."

The other shook his head wearily. "I'm afraid I don't know what you're talking about. You call me Larsen, but my name is Christiansen. If this is some kind of joke, then I'm afraid that it's on you."

I shook my head, aware that Neilson was watching me closely. "This is no joke, and believe me, I know who you are. Vlademar Larsen, ex-professor of Physics. As I was saying, Colonel Reddon believes that it is important you should be taken to England. He also told me to tell you that Minter still has the scar on his left hand where the sodium——"

The other suddenly uttered a half-strangled sob and clasped my hand tightly. "Minter. So it is true. You are from London. Oh God, I thought I would never live to see this day."

"Then you admit that you are Vlademar Larsen," said Neilson sharply.

"Yes. I am Larsen. I was afraid this might be a trap set by the Germans. That is why I denied it a moment ago. But the Germans could not possibly have known of what happened with Minter. It was all so very long ago, when we were two young students." Even as he was speaking, he had swung his legs to the floor and was pulling on his clothes hastily. "We were studying chemistry at the time and, like a fool, I dropped a piece of sodium, a large piece into water. There was an explosion, and Minter was burned on the back of his left hand by a piece of molten sodium." He turned to me. "When you told me about the scar, I still was not sure, but as soon as you mentioned sodium, then I knew."

"Good. We hope to get you out of Denmark very soon," I told him. "The Germans are looking for you too, that's why it was imperative that we should find you first."

"But how did you know where I was hiding? If you knew, then the Germans may also have found out."

"We located you less than five days ago," explained Neilson quietly, standing by the door. "There was a message from London asking us to keep a look out for you, although once we learned that the Germans were also trying to find you, it aroused our curiosity, so you might say that we have been searching for you for several months. How far the Germans are behind you, I'm not sure."

The other tried to smile, but it was a mere twisting of his thin lips and it served only to emphasise the deep shadows in his face and the dark circles etched beneath his eyes. It was only then that I realised what he must have come through during those past months, hunted and hounded by the enemy, trying desperately to keep on the move, knowing with a sick, sure certainly what his fate would be if the Germans, and especially, the Gestapo caught up with him. The relief at finding us there must have been almost overwhelming.

Outside, the silence was still there. I had the unshakable feeling that everything had gone just a little too easily for us, that our luck would shortly come to an end and then there would be hell to pay.

Reaching the others, we began to retrace our steps. Dark houses lay on all sides, and once, there was a bad moment as we were forced to remain crouched for several minutes while a German patrol moved within ten feet of us. Fortunately, they seemed to be merely enforcing the curfew and not looking for anyone in particular, otherwise I did not have the slightest doubt we would have been discovered. I felt duty and responsibility beginning to weight my mind. There were so many things which could happen now, all stemming from our discovery of Larsen. The truck? Had it been found during the interval. If so, would the Germans connect it with an attempt to find Larsen? When we reached it, nothing seemed to have been moved and at last, we were satisfied that it had escaped the notice of the enemy.

Very gently, I helped Larsen on board, then climbed up beside him. "The journey back isn't going to be pleasant." I told him quietly, "but we'll soon have you hidden away where the Germans won't find you until we've made arrangements to get you out of Denmark."

"Personal comfort means little to me, I assure you, now that I have the chance to get away." He settled himself down out of sight and a moment later, we moved off through the sleeping town.

I turned towards Neilson. "That patrol which stopped us on the way into Aastrup. If they meet us on the way back, they'll probably be more suspicious, especially if they find that nothing has been moved on the back of the truck."

"That thought had occurred to me," said the other quietly, dispassionately. "If they do become too suspicious, we'll have to kill them. I think they'll find that Hansen carries more in his truck than supplies for Herr Kommandant."

A quarter of an hour later, I saw what he meant. We were driving along one of the narrow side roads when there came the sound of shouts from ahead. From the back of the truck, it was impossible to see what was happening, but I guessed that another patrol—or perhaps the same one that had stopped us earlier that night—had signalled for Hansen to slow down. For a moment, I anticipated that he would do so, but instead, he must have jammed his foot down hard on the accelerator. The old engine responded gallantly to the demands made on it, and the truck leapt forward, shaking so violently that I expected it to come apart at the seams at any moment.

Almost before I realised what was happening, Neilson had moved forward, balancing himself carefully inside the swaying truck. In the darkness, I could see him pulling one of the smaller boxes towards the back of the truck, a wooden box which, judging from the effort needed to move it, must have been extremely heavy in spite of its size.

Then he had ripped off the top, plunged his hand inside, at the same time balancing it on the very edge of the truck with his body. A second later, there was a thunderous crash as we ploughed through a barricade which had been placed across the road. I was aware of splinters of wood flying through the air behind us, of harsh shouts and then the sound of rifle shots from somewhere close at hand. In the same instant, Neilson kicked the box overboard and threw himself back into the truck. Behind us, there was a vivid orange flash and a detonation that hammered at my ears. Bits of jagged metal whined through the air and one sliced through the canvas covering only scant inches above my head.

"What in God's name was that?" I gasped as soon as I had regained my breath.

Neilson grinned mirthlessly. "A box of supplies which Herr Kommandant would dearly have loved to get his hands on," he said with a terrible intensity in his tone. "It was full of grenades. I merely primed one just before

I pushed the box overboard. Somehow, I doubt whether they expected anything like that."

I felt myself shakng slightly as I settled back behind the other boxes. The ruthless, inhuman way in which the other had killed those Germans back there both shocked and appalled me, although I was forced to admit to myself, that it had been the means of saving us, that in the circumstances, it had been the only thing to do. But it was the dispassionate way in which Neilson had destroyed those soldiers which made me shiver.

We reached the farm a little before four o'clock in the morning. Already it was beginning to brighten in the east and the tall silhouettes of the trees stood out against the coming dawn. There was a fresh smell in the air that went down into my lungs like wine and a feeling in my mind that perhaps, after all, we were going to succeed in our mission.

All that we had to do now was to get Larsen to England in safety. There had been the unfortunate incident with the German patrol guarding the roadblock and in my mind there was not the slightest doubt that the enemy would scour the entire countryside looking for us. As yet, they probably had no idea that we had found Larsen. They would possibly put it down to another raid by the patriots. But it was something they could not allow to go unpunished.

"What are your plans now?" I asked Neilson, once we were inside the house.

"We must get in touch with London and tell them what has happened," he said thinly. "That may take a little time. At the moment, I do not know how they will get you out of Denmark. When we know that, we can make further plans. You will be safe here for the time being. Do nothing until you hear from us. If we do not come ourselves, Hansen will bring any messages. It is not going to be easy, but somehow, we will find a way."

He turned to Hansen. "I would hide your truck for a few days, just in case there were any survivors from that unsmiling as ever.

patrol. They may have recognised it, but I do not think so. Everything happened so quickly and it was completely dark."

Hansen shook his head. "That might be a foolish thing to do," he said. "If I do not deliver supplies to the Kommandant, awkward questions may be asked and as you know yourself, the Germans are better than most at putting two and two together. I do not think they will suspect me, but if they do, I will have a story ready for them."

"Very well." If the other disagreed with Hansen he gave no sign. His eyes were still dark and brooding as he threw Larsen a swift glance. "As for you, my friend. Remain out of sight—completely. There may be eyes watching out there. If they see you, even if they catch only the briefest glimpse of you, we are finished."

"I understand." The other sank down gratefully into one of the chair, and leaned back, his eyes closed. For the moment, it seemed as though all of the strength had evaporated from his body. He must have lived on the razor-edge of terror for too long, I thought watching him closely. Now that there was the chance of freedom, it was still just a little too much for him to really believe. He would not be sure until we landed in England. There, perhaps, I thought quietly, he might find the peace for which he had been searching so desperately, for so long.

CHAPTER SEVEN

Flight to Freedom

FOR close on a week, we remained in hiding, without a word from Neilson. At times, there was the suspicion in my mind that he was still trying to figure out some way of double-crossing us, some means of making sure that the Germans got their hands on Larsen, without implicating himself in the deal. The more I thought about it, the more the suspicion began to crystallise into something more definite and substantial. I had nothing to go on, merely a hunch that the other was taking just a little too long in getting a message through to London.

Every morning, without fail. Hansen went off to a secret rendezvous with the other, and when he came back it was always with the same story: The news had been passed to London, but so far, no instructions had been received from them as to our route of escape. And while all of this was going on, the Germans stepped up their search of the area. It was some measure of their determination to capture the men responsible for blowing up that road block, that they came not once, but five times to the farm, questioning Hansen, searching the house and outbuildings; and each time, we lay trembling in a secret hide-out beneath the barn. Fortunately, it was possible to see them coming for some distance and there was always plenty of time for us to get under cover.

Then, on the evening of the sixth day, Hansen came back with Neilson. This time the latter was alone. There was a faint smile on Hansen's face; but Neilson was as

"We have received instructions from London," he said, without preamble. "It will not be easy. Our escapade of last week had the effect of alerting a hornet's nest and we must find some way of slipping through it. A box of exploding grenades is not going to work this time, I'm afraid.

"Briefly, the position is that we have to get you to the coast, on board one of the fishing vessels. They say that it would be unwise to try to land a plane here and take you off that way, which might have been preferable all other things being equal."

"And once on board this fishing vessel," I countered. "What then? Surely you don't intend to sail us all the way to England. You'd never get more than ten miles off-shore and they'd nail you. If it were as easy as that, half the population of Denmark would be in England by now."

For the first time, a faintly derisive smile flickered around the other's lips. There was no humour in it and it seemed to make his feature's even more saturnine and evil than before. "Our orders are to rendezvous with a British destroyer two nights from now. They'll be waiting for us well outside Danish waters. What happens after that, is your concern."

"Will you be coming with us?" I asked.

He shook his head vehemently. "My place is here. After the war is over, there will be a lot for me to do in Denmark. We are going to build a new country here once the Germans are destroyed. The old order which existed before the war will be swept away and the people will rise and demand their share of the power. It will be they who govern Denmark, they who share in its wealth."

"All right, I get your point," I told him sharply. "There's no need now for a political speech. You and I, Neilson, are on opposite sides of the fence. We always will be, I'm afraid. But you're entitled to your own viewpoint just as much as I am to mine, I suppose. All I ask of you now is to get us safely on board that fishing vessel."

"Very well. We leave tomorrow. Unfortunately, we will have to travel during the daytime as well as at night if we are to reach the coast on time. I don't need to warn you of the dangers. The Germans are evrywhere. Your papers are in order and we have obtained some for Larsen. From now on, until you reach England, he is Carl Sveborg, an engineer, working for the Germans and on his way to Esbjerg. The rest of us are in a group travelling with him under orders from General Freiberg. Here are your work pemits."

I studied the card he gave me carefully. It seemed authentic and I wondered how under the sun they had managed to print it, to copy the signature so carefully. Even the seal looked authentic. With these, I thought, we at least have a chance.

The following morning, we went into Grindsted, an important rail junction. Everywhere there seemed to be German soldiers and out of the corner of my eyes, I noticed that they were checking identity cards, stopping people on the street, asking questions. Things were not going to be as easy as I thought.

"Keep with me and let me do the talking if we're stopped," said Neilson. "We make for the rail terminus, get the first available train out to Esbjerg. There's no point in trying to lay a false trail. The sooner we get there, the sooner we can contact the Underground there."

We were stopped by two armed soldiers at the very entrance to the station. I felt the familiar quiver of fear deep in my stomach, tightening the muscles into a hard knot; but I forced myself to remain indifferent to their presence.

"Your identity cards and work permits," snapped one of the men. He gave Larsen a hard glance, then turned his attention to Neilson as the other stepped forward.

Neilson spoke rapidly to them in German. "We're travelling to Esbjerg under orders from General Freiberg. You've heard of the General, I presume?"

The other nodded quickly, scrutinised the papers which Neilson handed over, then gave them back. There was a quick glance between himself and his companion which did not pass unnoticed and I saw that the mere mention of General Freiberg's name had been sufficient to cause them to alter their opinion of us slightly, that coupled with the fact that Neilson had spoken to them in fluent German and not in Danish as they had obviously expected.

"Your papers." The soldier turned to the rest of us. He glanced at them and then handed them back. "There is a train due to leave for Esbjerg in forty minutes," he said brusquely. "There is no telling when it will actually leave, these trains here cannot be relied upon to keep good time."

"Thank you." Neilson replaced the papers in his pocket and we walked slowly through the station entrance. It was several seconds before I realised that we had fooled the Germans, that we had been passed by them without any trouble. I felt some of my confidence returning as we bought our tickets and waited for the train to arrive. But even though we had passed that first test, I could still feel the tension beginning to mount as I noticed how many German troops there were on the station. Even the fact that most of them were not carrying rifles, failed to ease the clamping tension in my mind.

The train steamed into the station five minutes later and we found a compartment to ourselves. Three of the carriages were reserved for German military personnel and I noticed that all three were full.

"Why aren't we moving?" I asked ten minutes later, when we were still standing at the platform.

Neilson got up and went to the door of the compartment, looking along the narrow corridor. "There doesn't seem to be anything wrong," he said finally, coming back inside and closing the door behind him. "Must be some hold-up on the line. We'll be moving in a little while."

"Probably those two soldiers outside the station were suspicious after all and raised the alarm," suggested Larsen tightly. He was trembling a little, trying not to let the fear show through on to his face or in his voice.

"Nonsense. There's a perfectly rational explanation for it," I snapped. "Don't start getting ideas like that into your head. As far as the Germans are concerned we're a group of workmen on a perfectly legitimate journey. There's absolutely no reason why they should be suspicious. Now sit tight until we move off."

Five minutes later, with the train still standing at the

platform, the door of the compartment was slid open and two men stood framed in the doorway. One glance was sufficient. Gestapo! I fought down the tremor of fear and tried to eye them curiously, but without any apprehension. Beside me, I could feel Larsen shaking a little.

"Your papers!" said the first man harshly. He stepped into the compartment, the other man staying outside in the corridor.

Without a word, we handed them over, Neilson remaining quiet this time. The mere mention of General Freiberg's name would cut no ice with these men. Instead, they were more likely to hold us there until they had checked with the General himself and then there would be hell to pay when the word came through that he knew nothing at all of a group of engineers moving to Esbjerg on his express orders and why hadn't we been taken off the train and arrested right away?

"You're all going to Esbjerg?" The cold gaze flickered over us all, missing nothing, taking in every little detail. I shivered under that cold, inhuman gaze. These men left nothing to chance. It required only the slightest suspicion to cross their minds and we would be arrested, questioned, our papers checked, not as the soldiers outside the station had checked them, but thoroughly, in every detail. I knew that, no matter how good they were, how excellent were the forgeries on them, down to the last signature and seal, they would not stand up to that kind of scrutiny.

"That is correct," said Neilson calmly. Oh God, I thought frenziedly, how could the man sit there so calmly, so unruffled, in front of these men. But Neilson played his part well. Whatever else I thought of the man, he certainly did not lack courage.

"I see from your papers." The Gestapo official turned to Larsen, "that you are an engineer, going to work with the rest of these men at Esbjerg. Just what kind of engineer are you?"

"He's a structural engineer," said Neilson quickly. The Gestapo man was getting just a little too interested in Larsen for comfort.

"Let the man speak for himself," snapped the other sharply, whirling. His tongue lashed at Neilson savagely. "He has a tongue in his head, hasn't he? When I want an answer from you, I'll address you."

I'm sorry." Neilson sank back in his seat, face registering hurt at the other's remark.

"Now, to come back to my question. You are a structual engineer? Is that not so?"

"Yes," Larsen nodded. I could sense that he was holding himself under control with a tight effort of will, trying to force himself not to give us away by his actions. "They are building a new plant out there and I am to help in the work. It's all there on the work permit."

"I can read that for myself," murmured the other softly. He flipped the pages of the permit over with this thumb, not once lifting his gaze from Larsen's face. Was the other suspicious, I wondered, or merely curious, delighting in his power over a man who was obviously scared to death of him. "What kind of plant it is?"

Larsen hesitated for only the barest fraction of a second. "As far as I know, it's to be a processing plant for one of the big oil refineries," he said.

"I see." The other tapped his teeth thoughtfully with the permit, then handed it back with a sudden flourish. "Very well. Report to the local Kommandant when you arrive to get these permits stamped. You understand?"

We nodded in unison. The other stepped out of the compartment and slid the door shut, then vanished out of sight along the corridor. I sank back weakly in my seat, scarcely able to comprehend that we had come through that ordeal without our real identity being discovered. It still seemed incredible, little short of miraculous, five minutes later, when the train suddenly started.

"You think he suspected who we were?" asked Larsen, as we drew away from the station into the bright sunlight. "He may not have accepted our explanations."

"He accepted them all right," said Neilson confidently. "You were marvellous, my friend." He turned to me and went on enthusiastically. "Did you notice the way he brought in that oil refinery plant without so much as blinking an eyelid. You know, my friend, you ought to be with the resistance. I could do with a man who can lie like that to the Gestapo and not turn a hair."

"If you really want to know the truth," said Larsen weakly, "I was scared to death every moment he was questioning me. I felt sure he knew who we were and was merely playing with us like a cat with a mouse."

"If that had been the case, they would have arrested us there and then, and never have allowed us to proceed."

"Unless," I said softly, "they wanted to follow us at the other end, hoping that we'd lead them to another group of resistance workers."

Neilson rubbed his chin reflectively. "That's a possibility, of course," he admitted. "We must be careful when we reach Esbjerg."

The journey to Esbjerg took the best part of two hours. There was no sign of either of the two Gestapo agents on the train, but that did not help to allay the germ of suspicion in my mind. Alighting from the train, I threw a wary glance over my shoulder as we walked along the platform, but although several German soldiers got off the train and followed us, there was no sign of the two civilians who had questioned us on the train. By the time we had reached the ticket barrier and passed through I was feeling a little more at ease.

Slowly, wearily, I was content to follow Neilson. He seemed quite at home in Esbjerg and evidently knew the town well. I felt tensed, but not depressed. So long as our luck held, as it had on the train, we stood a reasonably good chance of getting on board that fishing vessel and then rendezvouing with the British ship.

"How long do we have to remain here?" I asked tightly, touching Neilson on the arm.

"Overnight, I'm afraid. We join the ship tomorrow afternoon, around five o'clock." His voice betrayed no emotion whatsoever.

"But will it be safe to stay here all that time?" I threw an anxious glance around me. There did not seem to be many soldiers in sight, but even that was not reassuring. The memory of those Gestapo men on the train was still fresh in my memory.

"The Germans are fools," muttered Neilson contemptuously. "They think that they know Denmark and the Danes so well. Even here, in Esbjerg, we have an excellent organisation. Have no fear. We shall be perfectly safe here. Many dozens of Allied prisoners of war and men who have been shot down over this country, have been sent back to freedom from here. There are places where men may be hidden even under the noses of the Gestapo."

"That makes me feel a little better," I said harshly. "But not much. I still have the feel of eyes watching me, boring into the back of my neck. The sooner we get off the streets, the safer I'll feel."

"Not long now," Nilson led the way along several narrow, winding streets, then into one which seemed longer than the rest, threw a quick look in both directions and led the way to one of the houses, a house which, from the outside at least, looked no different from all of the others.

"This is the place," he said quietly. "They should be expecting us."

He rapped sharply on the door three times, a pause and then once more. There was the brief rattle of a chain and then the door opened and Neilson stepped quickly inside, motioning us to follow."

I gave the man in the narrow passage a quick glance. Short, grey-haired, in his early sixties, I guessed, he had a worn, lined face, one which might have looked defeated if it had not been for his eyes. They seemed the only part of his features still alive. Brilliant and intense, they held the same expression as Neilson's did. A fanatical chill that sent a little shiver through me.

"I see that you made it without any trouble," he said dryly, shuffling into the room at the end of the passage and closing the door. "Everything is ready at this end.

Captain Andersen has been warned that there will be passengers tomorrow night. He sails with the tide a little after ten o'clock."

"Good," Neilson nodded. "We remain here tonight? There has been no trouble from the Germans?"

"None at all. A few patrols outside, but they do not bother with me. Why suspect a crazy old man who's mind they say is always in the past, who knows nothing of what is going on." "He gave me a shrewd glance. "That is a role which I have taken great pains to build up for myself. The Germans look upon me as a stupid old fool in his second childhood. A very excellent camouflage I can assure you. It saves me answering awkward questions and my house is not turned upside-down whenever the Gestapo think another search is due."

"That's all to our advantage," I said, nodding. "The less the Germans know about us, the better."

"You'll be quite safe here." The old man seemed quite sure of that and for some strange reason, I found myself believing him. "When you have had some food, you must sleep. You are not the first to stay here. There have been many others, passing through Esbjerg on their way back to England."

The meal that he provided a little while later was austere, but the food was good. I had a transient feeling of guilt, that we were taking what little the other had, leaving him with nothing for himself, but Neilson assured me that there was plenty of food where that came from, that the Resistance had their own methods of filling their larders, all with food stolen from the occupying forces. The Germans did not go short, and Neilson saw no reason why they should not help themselves whenever the opportunity presented itself.

After having eaten, I felt better. We were not out of the wood yet, but things were looking brighter than they had for some time: and Neilson now seemed genuinely determined to help us escape.

In spite of Neilson's assurances that there was little to

fear from the Germans, I spent most of my time during the remainder of that day, seated close to the window, watching the street outside; but it was almost dark before the German patrol appeared at the end of the street and began working their way slowly along it, obviously searching several of the houses. Neilson was at my side in a moment as I called out.

"We seem to have company," I said hoarsely, pointing, leaning back so that I could not be seen from the outside. "The worst kind. Looks as though they're cartying out some kind of search."

The other nodded, rubbed his stubbled chin, with a restrained deliberation that held a wealth of bitter comment. "If they decide to come here and search this house, they'll find us." I said with a harsh conviction. Outside, thirty yards away, a small group of soldiers came out of one of the houses. Two of them, rifles over their shoulders, hustled a half-dressed man between them, pushed him against the wall, arms held high over his head.

"Some poor devil they obviously suspect of being a patriot, or maybe they just want a hostage," growled Neilson.

"That isn't going to help us any," I told him fiercely. "They won't stop looking just because they've found him. I tell you they know we're here. This isn't just another routine search, it's too much of a coincidence for that."

"Don't worry, Vensen will take care of them. This is almost a monthly occurrence for him. Better come with me upstairs—quickly, all of you!"

The German patrol moved noisily along the street as I followed Neilson quickly up the narrow, winding wooden stairs. Larsen came close behind me, breathing heavily. At the top, we crouched in the darkness, pistols ready. If the Germans did burst in, if they began to search, put one foot wrong, several of them would die before they took us. We intended to sell our lives dearly. Even Larsen's face was grim and I noticed with a sense of surprise that the hand which held the heavy pistol was as steady as a rock. He would shoot if the time came, I reflected.

Suddenly, everything else forgotten, I started forward, clutching the pistol convulsively in my right hand. "What the hell is that stupid old fool doing?"

Down below, Vensen had rushed for the front door, wrenching it open, yelling loudly at the top of his thin, quavering voice: "Help! Help! British agents hiding in my house. Quickly!"

For a brief moment, the old man stood framed in the doorway and I had a bead on him with the pistol, my finger tightening on the trigger. It would have been the easiest thing in the world to have put a bullet between his shoulder blades, but two things stopped me from pressing the trigger. The instinctive knowledge that the shot would immediately bring the German troops into the house, that nothing would stop them then; and the stirring suspicion that there was a little more to this than met the eye. Neilson, if captured had only to say that the old man had sheltered us the whole of that day, and he would be shot with the rest of us. But first would come the torture at the hands of the Gestapo, to wheedle the truth out of all of us, and he would be less able to stand the torture than we would.

The idea that perhaps Vensen knew what he was doing was heightened as Neilson caught me quickly by the wrist. "Watch!" he murmured softly. "There's no need for that. Vensen has done this before. It isn't what you think."

A moment later, two German soldiers appeared in the doorway. Vensen was close behind them, acting the part of a frightened man to perfection, waving his skinny arms, lips mouthing words in a flood, a veritable torrent of warnings.

The two soldiers advanced into the downstairs room, rifles held at the ready. As yet, they couldn't possibly see us, crouched on the landing, but they had only to set toot on the bottom of the stairs and both would die with bullets through their brains. But there were all of the others out in the street, men who would come running, shooting, the moment any trouble started. I held my breath until it hurt in my lungs, the muscles of my arm and hand rigid and painful as I tightened my grip on the gun. Unsuspecting, the two men came a couple of feet further towards the stairs. Vensen was still shouting loudly, leaning backward a little, gesticulating to the others down the street.

Five seconds later, just as the first soldier was preparing to put his foot on the stairs, another man appeared in the doorway. He gave Vensen a withering glance. "All right," he rapped sharply. "There's no need to search this house. There's no one here."

"But the old man, Lieutenant. He said that there were British agents——"

"I know, I know." There was impatience in the Lieutenant's voice. "Some day you'll learn. This old fool will shout his head off every time he sees a patrol in the street. Twenty times at least, he has played the same old trick on us."

He whirled on Vensen, grasping the front of his shirt in a bunched fist. "But I warn you now, old man, the next time and I shall not be so lenient. The next time you try this, wasting my time, I shall take you down to Headquarters and if I do, you'll regret it, I promise you."

He barked a sharp order to the two soldiers at the bottom of the stairs, waited until they had stepped outside, then released his hold on Vensen's shirt. "Remember, old man. That was not an idle threat."

He slammed the door behind him, and a few seconds later, the sound of the patrol faded into the distance as they moved further along the street. Slowly, I rose to my feet, scarcely aware of the stabbing pains of cramp which probed through my legs. Exhaling quietly, I turned to Neilson. "I see now what you meant when you said he's done this sort of thing before."

The rest of the night passed uneventfully. In the room upstairs, I stretched myself out on the low bed, hands clasped behind my head, staring up at the ceiling. Outside, everything seemed quiet. Once, I heard the sound of a convoy of trucks roaring through the town and shortly before dawn there were the unmistakable sounds of the town coming to life. I had slept little through the night. Another twenty-four hours, my mind kept telling me; and if our luck held, we ought to be on board a British destroyer, safe from the enemy. But in spite of that, so much could happen during the next few hours.

"We must wait until the very last minute before we take you down to the harbour," explained Neilson. "The Germans are sure to be guarding the place. There have been too many escapes by sea. That's why we thought it best for you to remain here during the night. They will probably have searched the ship three times by now—and searched it thoroughly."

"And once we're on board, that will be the end of it?" suggested Larsen. "The ship will leave right away."

Neilson nodded soberly. "The ship will leave as soon as you are on board, because we shall see to it personally, that you do not go on board until the very last minute, but that will not—as you put it—be the end of it, I'm afraid."

"What do you mean by that?" I asked, looking up sharply. "I thought that once we were on that fishing vessel the Captain would take us out to rendezvous with a British destroyer."

"That is true," acknowledged the other quietly, "but unfortunately, there are such things as German coastal forces. They continually patrol the waters around the coast, boarding any vessels they consider might be carrying refugees, escaping prisoners."

"That's handy," I said bitterly. "Now you tell us. My God, why didn't you warn us this might happen?"

"Would it have made any difference to your plans if I had? I think not."

I shrugged hopelessly. "There's nothing we can do about it now. We've committed ourselves. I suppose that if Captain Andersen is prepared to take the risk of being boarded and having us discovered on his ship, then we ought to be prepared to take the chance too."

All that day, we lay hidden in the tiny house, with Germans moving on the street outside the windows. It was an uncomfortable feeling to know that the enemy were so close, that it only needed one of them to be a little more suspicious, a little more determined than the rest, to discover us. Slowly, the hours passed: the tension began to mount. In reality, it was doubtful that the Germans were any more watchful than usual; but to my tired mind, it seemed that there were far more of them abroad on the streets than we had encountered the previous day when we had arrived in Esbjerg.

When four-thirty came and Neilson indicated that it was time to go, I felt more at ease than at any time during the past forty-eight hours. Even though I knew that danger waited us on the streets, it made little difference. I tucked the heavy pistol into my belt, ready for instant use. If we were stopped and searched I would have no alternative but to use it. The death penalty was automatic for anyone caught carrying a weapon.

"All ready?" asked Neilson. His face still unsmiling, he stood near the door. I nodded, glanced at Larsen, saw the faint trace of fear on his face, the sudden stiffening of his shoulders.

"We're ready," I said harshly. "Let's get on board the ship. It wouldn't be courteous to keep the Captain waiting."

We stepped out into the street. There were still plenty of people around. Workers on their way home. Small groups of women, hurrying from the shops. It might have been an ordinary, everyday scene in Denmark before the war, had it not been for the armed men, walking watchfully among the crowds. Now that anti-Nazi feelings were running high, the German High Command had clearly decided to strengthen their forces here. I knew little of Danish politics at that time, apart from what little I had been able to pick up from Neilson and knowing his political outlook, I had little doubt that it was biased.

"Now whatever you do, try to act naturally," said Neilson quietly. "There is only one way to treat these Germans, with a contemptuous indifference. Above all, you must not show that you are afraid." He was looking directly at Larsen as he spoke and I knew what thoughts were running through his mind at that moment.

"I'll be all right," muttered the other defensively. "There's no need to worry about me."

"Very well then." Nelson gave a brief nod, patted the almost invisible bulge where the pistol reposed in his belt, and led the way along the street.

Twenty-five minutes, my brain kept repeating. Only twenty-five minutes and we should be on board that fishing vessel, ready to weigh anchor and sail out of Danish territorial waters. What happened after that was in the lap of the gods.

We approached the harbour by a circuitous route, deliberately taking the obviously less frequented streets. To all intents and purposes, we were merely three men, no different from the hundreds of others who worked in the town. Twice, there were bad moments when we ran into patrols, but although they gave us curious glances, we were not stopped and at exactly five minutes to five, we were inside the harbour.

I looked about me curiously, scarcely able to comprehend that it had been as simple, as easy, as that. There was no sign of any guards, but we did not pause to check on whether or not they were there. According to Neilson, they regularly patrolled the area, mainly after dark, and the fact that it was still broad daylight might have been a distinct point in our favour.

"Quickly," Neilson pointed. "There she is."

I started forward, with Larsen on my heels, but Neilson held me back. His fingers tightened into the flesh of my arm, biting with a steel-like strength through the thick cloth of my tunic.

"Not so quickly as that, my friend," he warned. "There may be Germans on board here." He paused for a moment, scanning the bridge of the tiny fishing vessel, then nodded in satisfaction as we caught a brief glimpse of an arm being waved. "All clear," he said quietly. "We can go on board now."

"Are these the two men?" asked Captain Andersen, eyeing us briefly. He was a tall man with a carefully-trimmed beard which gave him an almost piratical look. "You're on time. The Germans were here less than half an hour ago. I do not think they will come back now, they seemed satisfied, even though they almost destroyed my fishing equipment in the process."

"Then I leave you both in good hands," said Neilson quietly. For a moment, there was a brief smile on his face as he shook hands with both of us.

"Are you quite sure that you won't come with us?" I asked. "After all, if you stay here you'll be a hunted man. In England, I'm sure that Moller could find some work of importance for you."

"Moller!" He almost spat the word, then relaxed with an abrupt laugh that was a strangely ugly sound. "I'm afraid that Christmas Moller and I do not see eye to eye on anything. He and I could never come to terms. It is better that I stay here. There is still much for me to do. The war will not last for ever. Soon Hitler and his thugs will be destroyed and then there will come the time to build the new Denmark."

I nodded soberly. "I only hope that when that time comes, Neilson, you remember that a lot of the men who have died and are dying at this very moment so that Hitler may be destroyed, do not have the same political feelings that you do. Would it ask too much for you to respect their ideals too?"

"We shall see when the time comes," he said grimly. "That will be for the people of Denmark to decide for themselves. But until then, until the day of liberation, we must have only one aim in view. To kill as many Germans as we can."

I watched as he strode down the gangplank and vanished along the jetty. There was something about Neilson which was a little pathetic, I thought wearily. I wondered vaguely what kind of place he would have in the world once the war was over. Would he be a misfit, once of the minority, or would his kind try to run the world according to their ideals. Would they rise up to become as big a menace as Hitler was now?

Deliberately, I put the thought out of my head and followed Captain Anderson below. He brought out a bottle of wine, broke the seal and poured out three glasses. "Here's luck to this little venture of ours," he said quietly. His beard jutted out at a determined angle. "I suppose that Neilson warned you there's the possibility we may run into trouble before we rendezvous with the British destroyer. It is a remote possibility, but I think it only fair that you should be warned. They do have the unfortunate habit of stopping fishing vessels, particularly any fishing outside the territorial limit."

"We're in your hands, Captain Anderson," I said sombrely. "When do we cast off?"

He smiled. "We already have. Two minutes ago." He drained his glass at a single gulp and poured out another

I sipped mine slowly. From the taste of it, I guessed that the wine had also been taken from the Germans. Certainly it was far different from anything that the normal Dane managed to buy.

When we were well clear of the harbour, moving out into the encroaching twilight, we went up on to the bridge. There was a stiff breeze blowing off the sea and I noticed that there were severai other fishing vessels of all shapes and size heading in almost the same direction as ourselves. The sea was reasonably calm and there was only a slight sway noticeable on the boat.

"It should be dark in an hour or so," observed the Captain, casting a quick glance towards the west. "Then we can expect the coastal patrols to move among us. Usually they seem to pick a ship at random. It would obviously be far too difficult for them to stop and search every one."

"But if we're spotted moving straight out to sea, they'll give chase straight away," I said pointedly. "We'd give ourselves away."

"Perhaps. But whenever we have anyone on board to get away, word gets around and several ships move out to sea. Once again, the Germans cannot search us all and the odds are usually on our side."

Ninety minutes later, I saw what he meant. We were now well outside the territorial limits, heading out for the open sea. At least five other fishing vessels were within half a mile of our position, all heading in the same direction. Anderson pointed out the bow-wave of the approaching German vessel.

"Just as I thought. Here they come." In spite of the look of calm assurance on his face, he could not hide the trace of mounting excitement and apprehension in his voice.

For several minutes, the German ship nosed around the bunch of ships. I noticed the armament she carried and realised that we would not stand a chance if they ever opened fire on us.

"They're stopping one of the others," said Anderson, a moment later, peering through his binoculars. "This ought to give us the chance to slip away in the darkness. The others will keep the Germans occupied for the next three quarters of an hour."

Andersen's prophesy proved to be correct. In the darkness, with no moon and only a few visible through lowering cloud, we sailed north-west at a steady eight knots, finally keeping our appointment with the destroyer at seven minutes past midnight. Exactly four minutes later, we were on board and heading back towards England.

THE END